Old Sins Cast Long Shadows

Reviews

"Old Sins Cast Long Shadows" lives up to its fabulous title. It is not a book to be put down until fully read. Christina Brett takes you inside the heart and the mind of a cold and calculating female assassin, and the experience of being put there is not what you might imagine. You will see that murder *can* be an act that is cut-off from one's normal moralistic boundaries, and *may* be little more than the offshoot of an innate drive to force love and acceptance from a pathological parent."

Patricia Anne Dennison, author of "Stop the Voices" and "The Spell of Saint Cyril's Cemetery".

"Old Sins Cast Long Shadows" is an extraordinary new book about a hit-woman in organized crime, and so much more. It is so wonderfully different from anything you have ever read before, especially the main character, who you will love and dislike even after you have finished reading the book. "Old Sins Cast Long Shadows" will challenge you in so many ways – especially in the area of your sense of values. Long after you have put it down, you will savor the descriptions and accounts as they linger on in your mind for weeks"

Sam Yulish, PhD, author of "The Hesitant Psychic and Other Strange Stories", and "Where Have All The Hippies Gone?", and numerous educational publications.

Old Sins Cast Long Shadows

by

Christina Brett

Literally Publishing Limited

Old Sins Cast Long Shadows

by

Christina Brett

Published in the UK by Literally Publishing Limited
(www.literallypublishing.com)

ISBN 978-0-9554409-5-3

Literally Publishing Limited
The Covert
Main Street
Claydon
Oxfordshire
OX17 1EU
United Kingdom

Acknowledgments

It is rather incredible the amount of people involved in the making of a story, therefore, although I am grateful to many, I'll name those who had an impact in the development of this one.

Natasha Moore is a most important one, and I thank her for all the time spent with me shaping the story. Get the blue velvet dress for the big party, Nat! It will happen!

My friend of so many years Kem Pennington (*British by birth, English by the grace of God*) encouraged me and told me never to lose my faith when I thought that I had reached the end of my rope. Thank you for the information about the Ring of Kerry and for many other things...

My childhood friend in Uruguay, Dora de Concilis Quaglia, and her cousin in Rhode Island, Antonetta Quaglia, loaned me their name to use as Jackie's. See? I didn't forget this time.

I thank my children Lucy, Polly, Mikel, Christine, and Richard – and their families - for always being there and always showing interest in how the story was developing. A special word of thanks to my first grandchild Brett Maloney, *sportsman extraordinaire,* for lending me his name to use as mine.

Many thanks to Steven Ramírez for having faith in the story and for teaching me about script writing and about being patient.

The late Scott Rightley also encouraged me to keep writing and sent me millions of jokes to keep me smiling. I wish I could have thanked him in person before he passed away.

Jim and Laurie McAdams, newly-found friends and artists *extraordinaire*, designed the cover of this book and a movie poster that will surely win an Academy Award by itself. Thank you for your daily emails and words of confidence.

Last, but not least, to my sister Myrna Warnick and my brother Carlos Coirolo.

This book is dedicated to my mother Ilia B. Coirolo and my late father José M. Coirolo.

Prologue

Utah State Women's Correctional Facility – Draper, Utah, June 2005

Jackie Quaglia heard the prison doors closing behind her and she looked back at the strong gray door that had held her for so many years. The Board of Pardons had denied her parole so many times that she felt more than once the desire to just giving up and tell every one of its members to go to hell or go jump in the Great Salt Lake, a few miles northwest of the prison.

Through the glass doors she could see two of the guards that had become not exactly her friends, but as close as guards can become to inmates. They waved at her and she waved back. She wasn't sorry she'd never see them again, but at the same time, a bit of something close to pain touched her chest.

She wasn't going to miss the ugly square building, the large lawn area in the back, the gray cells with narrow slits for windows, or the bad food – but that had been her life for the last fifteen years. She had made friends and enemies, she had had fights with some and crying bouts with others. She had done the laundry, worked in the kitchen and in the library, had been the teacher's assistant to the GED program, she had been feared by some and called "sis" by one. She had been queen and peasant.

But it was over. She was free and she'd never come back to that place, she'd never crossed its "revolving doors" again, called that way as a sick joke by those who kept coming back a month after their release.

Looking around, she saw the black Lincoln Town car that was waiting by the main gate, motor idling. *Wow,* she thought, *they didn't use to be this fancy!* When she got closer, a man of about thirty-five got out and came around to the passenger door to open it for her. Good heavens!, it was Dino! Her father's chauffeur had been about twenty-three when she took her last drive to O'Hare airport with him. She was on her way to Utah for another one of her jobs for her father. Dino's English was broken at the time and she always spoke Italian to him. His last words to her that day had been *"Take good care of yourself, Signorina Jackie, I'll be waiting for you when you get back."*

But she never did. Until today, and he was waiting for her as promised.

"Dino!," she said and hugged him. As he didn't respond, she looked up and saw the tears in his eyes. He smiled, however, and said with a broken voice, "If you tell anyone about this, I'll deny it."

She laughed and squeezed his arm. "Our secret," she whispered. He took her elbow and guided her towards the open door. She went in and patted the fine upholstery, asking Dino to sit with her.

"I'd love to, but we better get out of this place. It gives me the creeps."

"It should!" she said, "OK, drive on and we can stop somewhere and have a chat." He closed the door and walked to the driver's side of the car. She looked out of the window, now covered with the dark glass, and saw for the last time in her life, the gray walls of Utah State Prison. The imp living within her soul thought about putting down the window and giving it the birdie, but she was tired of fighting the system so she just looked ahead and asked Dino to get going.

Jackie was wearing a beige and dark green two-piece suit that had been mysteriously sent to the prison for her a few weeks before her release. High heels, fine stockings and even a gold locket were part of the ensemble, as well as silk underwear – something that she hadn't seen in ages. She felt pretty good wearing real clothes, and when she and Dino sat in the lounge of the Salt Lake Hilton an hour after her release, she looked around the place and almost pinched herself. Actually, she didn't to pinch herself because she was afraid of this being a dream and she didn't want to wake up.

Dino was just looking at her, and Jackie remembered that he had been half in love with her way back then when he was driving her to and from the airport every time she had a job outside of Chicago. She gave him her killer smile, which she hadn't lost in all of these years of hell. "So, Dino, tell me what's happening with you and everybody else."

He waited for the waitress to deliver the drinks that they had ordered and then said, this time in an

English with just a slight Italian accent, "As you know, after Tony died you were the heiress apparent, but with you being here an all, your cousin Marco became the boss. He never did very well, Jackie, and the family lost a few…'cases'… that should have been won if you had been there." He lifted his glass and said *'salute, cara'* (cheers, darling) and she did the same, then both took sips.

He then continued, "Marco took a bullet in the spine back in '99 and has been confined to a wheelchair ever since. He can't move his legs and that makes his job even more difficult." His dark brown eyes linked with green ones. "Everybody is waiting for you, Jackie. We have men who don't want to be told what to do by someone who can't even wiggle his toes – you know how it is…", she knew, "and during the last meeting in the big house, it was decided that the post is yours. You have to go to Chicago, and it was provided in your parole that you will."

Jackie knew that they had held an attorney, one of the best in Chicago – fifteen years too late, she mused - to handle all the dealings with the Adult Probation and Parole Department in Utah, and she was put under the supervision of the same office in Illinois, who took the attorney's word that Jackie would be living in Elmhurst, a few blocks where Tony's house was located. No names or relationships had been given to the AP&P and because they very seldom check on anything, courtesy of the overworked government and state agencies, all had gone through without a cinch.

She looked at her drink. "So," she said after a moment, "back to the old life again."

Dino blinked. "You don't seem to be very convinced."

She looked at him and sighed. "Dino, I was in that hell for fifteen years, and I swore when I left – a couple of hours ago as a matter of fact – that I'd never go back! No matter what…I'm getting out of this life!"

Dino looked around the lounge as if waiting for an answer to suddenly appear on the walls. "And how are you going to avoid it?"

"That's my problem, Dino, and the less you know, the better off you are. I have plans for myself; I have everything set up to disappear and nothing or anybody is going to stop me. Maybe I shouldn't be telling you this, but you and I have been friends for a long time."

"That goes without saying, Jackie…but you know that they'll find you."

"No, they won't. I can assure you. I'll meet with them tomorrow when we get to Chicago, just as planned, and they'll think I'm with them, but as soon as my plans come together I'm history. I have all the money I can use in two lifetimes, and if for some reason I ran out I'll work…but I'll be damned if I'm going to fulfill Tony's wishes after he's dead. As far as I'm concerned, he put me in prison and never did a damn thing to get me out. There was a time when

I'd have escaped if I had the chance, but he never helped me. Now it's my time and as far I'm concerned, he can rot in hell!"

Dino didn't know what to say, but knew that she was speaking the truth. He also knew that the words they were exchanging at that moment would never leave his soul, and Jackie had a friend forever in him.

The United Airlines flight landed in Chicago with a soft *bump-bump* on the runway, making Jackie open her eyes. She, so used to flying before, had not set foot in an airport or in a plane for fifteen long years and the three-hour flight from Salt Lake City International Airport to her familiar O'Hare had been too long for her taste. Her first-class seat next to Dino's was comfortable and the booze provided by the starry-eyed flight attendant had not erased her feeling of foreboding that engulfed her. Why? *Beats me!*, she said to herself when she wondered why she didn't want to go to Chicago. But deep inside she knew. That was the city where she was born and grew up, where Tony had taught her to kill without remorse, where she had enjoyed quiet days in her Lake Shore Drive penthouse sitting in a balcony that faced the placid Lake Michigan and had dreams of living in Ireland with Aidan.

Aidan. She wondered what had become of him and whether he'd think of her...Ha!...Probably not. When one leaves a man with high hopes and disappears into thin air the only thoughts he probably had for her would be filled with hate.

She shook her head. Would she contact him? Shaking her head she thought no, of course not! He was no doubt married to a sweet colleen, someone who shared his love for animals and a quiet life in his beloved Ring of Kerry. The cabin of the plane was suddenly draped in mist…No, it wasn't mist, it was tears that filled her eyes and prevented her from seeing straight.

Dino looked at her. "Jackie! What's the matter? You are crying!"

"I'm an idiot, Dino…sorry."

He took her hand in his. "No you are not, Jackie girl…and it's OK to cry!" It was his turn to say this.

She smiled at this sweet giant of a boy who had become a grown man during her absence. "*Grazie, carissimo…*I'm OK, really."

He kept holding her hand and looking at her, and she was grateful for his friendship – probably the only friend she had at this moment.

They stood up when the doors of the airplane opened and started to leave the cabin. Because they didn't have luggage – Dino had taken just a carry-on for his trip to Salt Lake City, and she had put her meager belongings in a large handbag that was hanging from her shoulder – they cleared the airport and were soon outside hailing a cab.

Jackie's eyes didn't tire of seeing Chicago once again. So many new buildings in the far away Loop!

New parks and shopping centers all over the place...and always, everywhere, the rush of people in and out of cars and buildings. That never changed.

In the cab that was taking them to her old house Dino asked her, "And what is the first thing that you are going to do now that you are free, *cara?*"

"I am going to buy me a cellular phone... They boggle my mind!" and as an afterthought, she added, "Of course, I don't have anyone to call...so I'll just keep calling Pop-Corn I guess..."

"Pop-Corn" Dino's face was puzzled.

"A long time ago that was the number you called to find out the time of day. You're too young to remember..." and they both laughed.

They went straight to the Big House, as Tony's house had been called, and she waited in the old office for her cousin Marco.

He showed up a moment ago in a wheelchair pushed by someone who had probably taken growing vitamins in his milk bottle. Marco looked at her cousin and smiled, a sincere smile, she saw, but then, why not? She and Marco had been good friends since childhood and she remembered the time when she had to kill a member of another family in order to get him out of a big mess.

"Marco! Good to see you..." She went to him and kissed his thin cheek.

"And you too, Jackie. How you doin'?"

She shrugged her shoulders. "Well, nice to be out here, that's for sure…"

"I have always thought about you, many times during these past fifteen fucking years, kid. I'll never forget that you helped get me out of a jam more than once…"

She laughed. "All in a day's work, Marco." She sat down and was now at eye level with her cousin. He looked haggard, was thin, and she noticed that his hands shook a little. "Now, tell me what's going on."

He crossed his hands on his lap and looked at the Goliath that had pushed him into the room. "It's OK now, Joey. Go and have a coffee break."

Joey took a long look at Jackie and moved slowly out of the room. "Where did you get him? Out of Dracula's coffin?", she asked.

Marco laughed. "I can see that you haven't lost your wicked sense of humor!"

"Thank goodness for that! I'd be climbing the walls if I had."

"I know what you mean, kiddo. So, the thing is…I'm the boss now. Tony's legacy is supposed to be alive and well, but to tell you the truth, it's barely making it."

Jackie looked at him and realized that he wasn't bitter. *I'll be damned,* she thought. "And what do you want me to do?"

"Take over. Tony always wanted *you* to be his successor, but those years in the clink made me the one... but I can't do it; the men in the organization refuse to be led by a cripple and, the truth is, I don't feel like doing it."

Jackie looked around the room. When this was Tony's office, heavy wood bookcases filled the room, his enormous desk was near one of the windows, and she could visualize the branches of the big oak tree hitting the windowpanes.

"Marco...I'd prefer not to be the one. You know damn well that if I'm caught and sent back to prison they're going to lock me up and throw away the key."

"No, they won't Jackie..."

She slapped her hand on her knee and stood in front of her cousin. "Of course they will! What's the matter with you? I'm on fucking parole, Marco. Get it through your head!"

His hand went up like a policeman's in a busy intersection. "Calm down, Jackie. Everything has been arranged so that you'll...'die'...in an accident or due to some illness. We'll send the death certificate to the State, and the attorney will send it to Utah and they'll take you off their books."

"Die? I'm going to *die?*"

"Yeah...well, no, not literally...we'll fake your death. Everything will be a fake so that Jackie Quaglia will no longer exist..."

Jackie was going to say something when a little light lit her brain. Wait a minute...if she was going to 'die', then she could be home free. All the plans she had would be done for her. Of course, she'd still disappear once all the work was done, but Marco didn't have to know this. She sat again and waited a moment before she asked the question. "And there won't be a trace of Jackie Quaglia?"

"No trace. You'll be cremated, and a new identity will be born that day."

"How are you going to do this? Have you ever heard of *fingerprints?* What do you plan to do about them?"

"There's a doctor in Detroit...he has done the job for others before. He burns your fingertips..."

"Ouch! That probably hurts as much as flogging!"

"You won't feel it, Jackie. We'll ask him to put you under, and when you wake up your fingers will be as smooth as a baby's bottom."

Those plans certainly fit her secret ones. Still... "Marco...whose idea is this?"

"Mine, mostly…but also Tony's. He had some notes made up, and he also spoke with his lawyer that once you came back he wanted you to consider this possibility."

"You know, Marco…for that you need a doctor and a funeral home. Am I stupid to ask if you have someone paid to do that?"

"Yes, we have someone in payroll…"

"Of course," she said in a whisper, and added, "What about my face, Marco?"

"What about it? It's still gorgeous. Nobody would tell that you are 42…but if it makes you feel better, he can do something while he's at it."

"And how much do you trust that doctor?"

"A lot. He has been working for us for over ten years now and he has been loyal. But then, the fee we pay him keeps him quiet." He looked at the ceiling. "That and the fact that he knows his entire family will be wiped out if he ever beeps a word."

"Things never change around here."

"So, you see," continued Marco, "you'll be safe."

She walked towards the window and looked outside without really seeing anything. She was there for so long that was almost shocked to hear Marco say, "What d'you say, Jackie?"

She thought about it for just a moment. "All right. Give me time to get used to idea of being free, and settle in my apartment. By the way…what happened to it?"

"Gianni and his family have it. Do you wann'it back?"

She looked back at the tree outside of the large window. If everything went right she would be out of the country within a month, so why take the apartment from Gianni who had always been quite decent with her?

"No, it's fine. Let him have it. I'll stay in Elmhurst…"

"What about your furniture and shit?"

"My belongings are not *shit*, Marco. Leave them there. I'll go to the storage place and get a few very personal things I have there, and I'll decide what to do with the rest." There were things to plan, and the first on the list was to send her old passport to be renewed – that was the passport she had under the name of Jackie Millard, the same one she had used to go to Ireland to visit Aidan so many years before.

She smiled when she looked at Marco again. "OK, I'll go along with those plans . When can we meet with the rest of the family?"

They talked for another hour or so and finally Jackie left for the house in Elmhurst, a big Tudor that had been her uncle Sal's home before he died.

"See you soon, Marco. Stay well.'

He kissed her back and rolled his chair to the door with her. She saw the giant Steve sitting by the door and wondered if he had heard any of the conversation that took place inside. Didn't matter, really. She was going to be free from all this shit soon and should start looking forward to it.

That night, guarded by at least four burly men, a cook, and a maid in the house in Elmhurst, Jackie sat in the sitting room that was adjacent to her bedroom, put her feet up on an ottoman, and sipped her Remy Martin. The drink had been one of the things she had missed most when she first got to the State Prison in Utah – well, that and her silk underwear, the delicious food, and her clothes –and so many nights she'd lie in her narrow cot looking at the bottom of the upper one, and dreamed of its incredible taste! Shaking her head, she looked around the room and pinched herself. Yes, she was out of prison, she was in one of the many houses that the family owned in the Chicago area, and she was sipping her favorite drink after enjoying a great dinner cooked by the Mexican cook that ruled the kitchen with an iron hand.

She closed her eyes and, although she didn't want to dwell on the ghost of seasons past, she thought of her previous life.

CHAPTER ONE

It was one of those summer days when not only clothes stick to bodies but also the asphalt seems to melt, making one wish to be in a cabin in the woods in the middle of Wyoming. But this wasn't Wyoming: It was Boston, and the heat was unbearable although it was almost seven in the evening.

The woman sitting in the front seat of the rented car was taking sips of water from a bottle on the seat by her; she was wearing dark glasses and her age was in the late twenties, with beautiful auburn hair and one of those faces that could launch a thousand ships.

Her left arm lifted again to look at her watch, an expensive Rolex that had been Tony's present three years ago. Tony. She was in hot Boston today because of him. He was supposed to send Carlo or someone else to do this job, but because of some screw-up in his system, she had to cover for Carlo. Her thoughts kept wandering, and she looked at her watch again. Damn the man! Where the hell was he? It was 7:14 PM and he should have been out of the factory over half an hour ago.

Her right hand caressed the pistol she had on the seat covered with a white shawl. As soon as this job was over she was going to take a vacation somewhere cold, like South America. She had heard that Buenos Aires was the place to visit, or maybe fabulous Punta del Este, in tiny

Uruguay. She was going to sit in front of the Atlantic and watch the soft winds move the palm trees. Well, she hoped there were palm trees down there too. Yes, she'd do just that, and was not going to tell Tony a word about it.

Seven minutes later she saw the side door of the factory open and a medium height man came out. He was wearing a blue suit, but when he closed the door behind him, he took off his jacket and put it over his arm. With the other hand he carried a briefcase. He walked slowly, as someone who was tired of being tired.

With a quick look around, the woman took the pistol and aimed at him. There were no cars or other people in the street. This was going to be an easy shot. Aiming, she fired two bullets that hit the man in the neck and the other right behind his ear.

There was no blood spilt and nobody heard the noise because the gun was equipped with a silencer. If anyone had been watching, all they would have seen was a man who fell on the sidewalk, arms outstretched, the contents of his briefcase scattered all around him. Five seconds later, the woman started the car and headed east towards Logan International Airport.

CHAPTER TWO

The man in the Hertz office at the airport looked at Jackie and thought she was a real looker. "Everything OK, Miss?"

She gave him a quick look and nodded. "Hot enough for you?" Why do people say that? It was the stupidest question she had ever heard. The man wanted to chat, but was getting nowhere fast. She looked at him and something in her eyes told him that this wasn't either the place or the time.

"So... you returning the vehicle now?"

"Looks that way, doesn't it?" she hissed back.

"I just wanted to know if you wanted to keep it a few more days."

"No, thanks."

"Sure?"

She turned around and looked at him. "Look, I am in a hurry. I don't need the car any more, thank you very much. Here is my credit card, charge it and let me go!"

"Yes, Miss…" he read the name in the fake card, "…Taylor. Like Elizabeth. You look like her too." She didn't. He ran the credit card, made her sign the receipt, and watched when she walked out of the office. He smiled to himself, moved his head from left to right and said, "They all act like that, but when the time comes…"

If he had walked out with her he would have heard 'jerk!' repeated many times under her breath. She walked fast towards the terminal that had Tony's plane to go back to Chicago. The plane was a sleek Lear A31 whose pilot, Rick Milano, cared for as if it were his child.

Rick was standing outside, waiting for her. She climbed the ladder fast and he followed.

"Everything OK, Jackie?"

"All is well, Ricky… let's get out of here. I hope the plane is cool."

"It will be as soon as we take off. Vincent is in there with your drink ready."

He got a bright smile in return, and after making sure that everything was in place, he went into the cockpit. Jackie sat in one of the plush seats of the airplane and soon Vincent came with her drink. Vincent was deaf and mute and had been in Tony's employ for at least forty years. He had known Jackie when she was born, had played with her, and had taught her to ride a bike because Tony was too busy to do it himself. Jackie loved him as if he were her favorite uncle and had learned sign language because of him.

She took the drink and he sat by her, both fastening their seat belts following Rick's instructions.

"You OK, kid?" he signed.

"Fine, Vin. This was an easy one."

"You look upset."

"No, not upset, it's this blasted heat, and the jerk at the Hertz office put me in a bad mood."

Vincent laughed and signed, "Temper, temper…"

She looked at him. "Vin… of all the time that you have known Tony… did he ever do anything that wasn't for his own selfish good?" She had been wondering about that while sitting in the car waiting for her victim to show up.

The older man looked out of the jet window and saw the terminal and the airport buildings running backwards until the plane lifted off. His lips were pursed together.

"Once, a long time ago, maybe even before you were born, Tony and I had gone over to Detroit to see the family of one of his men that had been gunned down. The man had been an asshole as far as his family was concerned. He beat his wife and kids and the house they lived in was not suitable for anything but rodents. Tony saw the place and talked to the woman for over an hour, and when we left we went straight to a new building that had apartments for sale near Ann Arbor... He actually made all the arrangements to buy one of the apartments for Mrs. Cannelli and her kids, found her work at GM and as far as I know, paid for the kids college over at Michigan State. She changed her name to Cannell."

Jackie had left her glass on the little table by her seat. "You're kidding! He didn't even try to sleep with her?"

He laughed and moved his head from side to side. "Not that I know of, and I was with him all the time in those days."

"Amazing!" she said aloud, and he read her lips.

"Quite amazing!" He leaned back in his chair. "Does that answer your question?"

"I guess... You know Vin, I have been thinking about quitting..."

"You have?" He sat up to look at her from a better angle.

"Yes. I'd like to lead a normal life. I don't have any friends to call and chat, to go to the mall, or to vacation with. When I was growing up, I was the only kid in school that couldn't ask her friends to sleep over, or go to camp... Then, as soon as I turned seventeen and Mom died Tony started to train me for this life." She looked out of the little window and saw clouds like cotton candy underneath the jet. "Every time I finish a job I see myself going to the big house to tell Tony that this is it… but it never happens. I don't have the guts."

The older man took her hand. He kept holding it for a while, and then let it go to speak to her. "Jackie… first of all, you are the gutsiest woman I have ever met. Don't ever say you don't have guts because you are doing yourself an injustice. If you are serious about this, if you really want to quit, maybe I can help you. I can be with you when you tell Tony."

She smiled at him. "You are such a darling, Vin. As far as I'm concerned, you are my real father. You and Mattina were always there for me, especially after Mom died…and as being with me when I tell Tony…ha! I'll need the entire First Division with me to face his wrath."

He made a vague gesture with his hands as saying maybe, maybe not, and then signed "We love you, kid. Never forget it."

"I know. And I adore the two of you, don't YOU ever forget it."

They held hands for a while, and when he got up to get her another drink, Jackie put her head against the seat and closed her eyes.

What she had told Vincent was true. Tony Quaglia, her father, had trained her to kill without remorse. She came from a family that was in the "revenge business", as Tony usually said, and in that business only a brain is necessary. One could leave the heart at home, or better yet, in the crib.

When Jackie Quaglia was seventeen her mother died of a heart attack while they vacationed in Michigan's Upper Peninsula. They came back to Chicago and after the funeral was over, Tony had called her into his study.

"Sit down, kid, sit over here by me." Jackie had been in his study just a few times in her life. Tony's study was off limits to her and her mother.

He had told her that he knew she was sad because of her mother's death, and that she could take a vacation somewhere if she wanted.

Jackie had looked at him. "I don't know anybody, Tony. Where would I go?"

His shrug told her once more that he didn't give a hoot about her.

"I don't know… To Canada, to Mexico, to Europe… There's lots of foreign countries out there. You can ask Vin and Mattina to go with you."

Jackie remembered looking out of the window to see the large oak tree where she used to climb when she was a child. "No, Tony… I don't think so. I think I'd like to go to college. I could go to Northwestern because my grades in school are high, or maybe to a school in the East coast…"

"University? Why the hell you wanna go to the university? I never went nowhere, and I'm doing just fine!" He had been furious at the thought.

"I want to go to university because I like to study, Tony. What else am I going to do? Find me a husband, get married and have nine kids in eight years?"

"Don't you talk to me like that, Jackie! I'm your father!"

"I'm not saying you are not! I just want to do something useful with my life."

"And you will. This is why I brought you here." To her amazement, he had offered her a glass of Scotch from his overflowing bar. She refused it but he made her take the glass.

"Drink up, Jackie. You are a grown woman today." At seventeen?

She knew better than to refuse one of his requests, so she took a small sip first. The beverage burned her throat and stomach and she coughed. "Come on, Jackie, no daughter of mine is going to be a sissy!"

After the coughing stopped, her eyes were red and her cheeks flushed. He was sitting on the side of his desk, an enormous piece of furniture that belonged in a castle somewhere, not in one of Chicago's best neighborhoods.

"Jackie…" he continued, "You are my only kid, and I'm not getting any younger."

Right, she thought.

"I want to train you to someday take my place within the family."

Her eyes widened. The family actually consisted of more than ten names, each name an individual who had at least twenty people under him. Tony was the capo, the man in charge of all of them.

"Tony, you forget a teeny-tiny detail here: I happen to be a girl."

"So what? You're my daughter, and any daughter of mine is considered more than a girl."

She almost laughed at her father's words. "Right. And do you think that the rest of the family is going to accept me just like that?"

"I don't give a flying fuck about what the rest of the family thinks! Whatever I say goes. I know it, you know it, and they know it." He served himself another Scotch. "I am going to start training you, first with the bookkeeping part of the business, later on I want you to learn how to use a gun, and mebbe when you turn twenty-one I can start you going out with some of the boys."

Jackie put the glass on his desk. "Tony, this is a crazy idea. Those men are never going to accept me, especially the Rossis. Can you see Benito Rossi taking orders, or even listening to ideas from a woman? He'll have me killed before I can say Jack Robinson."

"Who's Jack Robinson?"

She moved her head. "Nobody, Tony, it's just a saying."

"Oh. OK, back to what I was saying. You're gonna sit with Marcelo every day and learn the procedures. You've got to know the name of my companies, what each does, and the names of their managers. Then, you can start with the real estate holdings. That's the most important lesson in this here course." As always, he hadn't listen to her. He took a long sip of his Scotch. "Now, Jackie, to start your training…" but she interrupted him, "Tony, I didn't say I wanted to do this."

"It don't matter what you want, young lady. What d'you want? To have everybody laughing at Tony Quaglia because he can't tell his fucking daughter what to do?"

"Quit swearing! You never swore in front of Mom, at least respect her wishes if nothing else!"

Tony knew she was right. "OK, OK… I feel like a damn sissy talking with you."

"Then don't talk to me, Tony. Let me go to college and I'll be out of your hair."

"I don't want you to be out of my hair, dammit! I don't want you out there by yourself because I have a million enemies and I'm afraid someone will try to get to me through you. Is that clear now?"

They had argued and fought for half an hour, and when Jackie realized that she was losing, she decided to let it go. It was no use arguing with Tony because if he didn't win, he started to yell making life around him very difficult. She'd go along with his wishes, would sign for correspondence courses in some university that offered them, and let life continue.

Vincent's touch in her arm made her open her eyes, letting go of her thoughts.

"You look tired, kid."

"Not physically tired, just fed-up, Vin... what do you have here?" She took the glass that he was offering her.

"It's called water, and this is an aspirin for your headache."

She laughed but took the offered glass and pill.

"See what I mean?" she told him after taking the pill and water, "what would I do without you?"

At that moment Rick lit one of the red lights above their seats, which meant for them to get ready for landing. Vin sat again by her, and they felt the landing gear being lowered and the aircraft started its descent over Chicago.

Once in the airport, Jackie and Vin rushed through the tarmac to a waiting limo. The driver, a young man in his mid-twenties, greeted both and opened the door for them.

"Gratzie, Dino." said Jackie. She always spoke Italian to him.

"Signorina…" he said and touched his cap.

The drive through Chicago busy streets didn't do anything to calm her nervousness; every time she had to go out of town for a hit, she spent at least two days in her apartment on Lake Shore Drive without seeing anyone, not even her father.

"Donde, Signorina, a la casa grande?" He wanted to know if she was going to Tony's house.

"No, Dino, a la mia casa, per favore." She'd wait until the next day to see her father.

"Bene."

She didn't want to go to the big house in Elmhurst and face Tony. She'd just go to her own place and stay there. After any hit, she wanted to rest and clear her mind from the kind of work that, although it was making her very rich, she was tired of doing. She wanted the freedom of coming and going without guarding her back; she wanted to be able to have friends, not foes. She wanted to be herself.

When the big car stopped in front of her building, she got out after kissing Vin and waving good-bye to Dino and walked fast towards the entrance. Mr. McMillan, the doorman, greeted her with his usual cordiality. "Good morning, Miss Quaglia. Back so soon? I watered your plants last night, thinking you'd stay away longer, so don't give them anything for another week."

She stopped at his ornate wooden cubicle that looked more like a pew in a cathedral. "Hello, Mr. McMillan! Yes, it was a fast one, and I thank you for keeping an eye on the plants. How's Mrs. McMillan? Better, I hope?"

"Yes, much better. Getting ready to our annual visit to Scotland…"

"How lucky for you! Let me know before you leave."

"I shall. Is there anything you need today?"

"No, nothing, thanks. I have to do some paperwork and then I want to sleep for seventeen days…"

"You work too hard. You should be having fun instead."

"Yes, but who's going to pay the bills?" As if she had any bills to pay...but that was the answer expected from someone who worked as hard as she.

He was already opening the elevator doors for her, and stood aside when she entered the box. "Right, right. Well, stay well Miss Quaglia!"

"Thanks, same to you and your wife."

He touched the tip of his hat as the doors closed. Jackie owned the building and lived in the penthouse, a large, airy, apartment that faced Lake Michigan. She never got tired of sitting in the balcony to watch the lake, with its changing moods and colors. The building had nine floors, with two apartments in each. She had kept the penthouse because it was very secure and because it had its own elevator that opened into a small hall by the apartment's front door. Tony had seen the building when she decided to buy it, and soon sent two large carpenters to put a new door that would be more secure than the thin film she had before.

Jackie had built a safe in one of the closets in her bedroom. The safe was camouflaged with a dark 'headache wallpaper' as she called it, and one had to know the safe was there in order to find it. The safe had two guns in it, a 9mm Beretta and a Colt 45 automatic, some cash, and all her fake IDs provided by Tony.

Jackie felt safe in her apartment and nobody had ever tried to break into it. Her alarm system was one of the best, and because of the address, the police would came running when needed. She wasn't afraid of burglars, the ones from the street who go into houses looking for a hefty loot, but of the many members of other families who were against her because she was a woman and better than any of them. One of the other family heads, Benito Rossi, had sworn that she was going to be brought down because his two sons should be in line for Tony's position when he died. What he didn't know is that when that time came, Jackie was going to quietly disappear, as she didn't want to be connected any more with the lot of them.

After cleaning her 9mm Beretta used in Boston, Jackie put it away in the safe, moved clothes to be in front of it, and went to the bathroom to fill the tub with lavender water for the longest bath in history. Her stereo system had speakers piped into the bathroom and soon Vivaldi filled the entire apartment. A glass of Remy Martin on the tub border completed the scenario.

Inside of the tub, her glorious hair tied back with a ribbon, and lavender bubbles covering her to her neck, she relaxed, sipping her drink every few minutes and thought about her first job. It had been terrifying to know that she had to terminate somebody's life with a bullet, and when she got word from Tony that she was needed in his office she came down the stairs not knowing that she would soon become an assassin for her father.

She opened the heavy door and saw her father standing by the large window, his hands clasped behind his back.

"You wanted me, Tony?"

He turned around and faced her. "Yeah, kid...Sit down here," and he moved a chair in front of his desk. She sat and looked at her watch. She had been working on a final exam for one of her classes and didn't want to be distracted with some of Tony's long speeches.

"What is it, Tony? I am busy."

"Busy? What is so important that you can't take a moment to speak to your father?"

She couldn't say that she was preparing a final exam because he didn't know she had been taking classes, so she shrugged and gave him the answer he was expecting of her. "I was reading an incredible story about Al Capone, Tony... Did you know that...?"

But he interrupted her. "Not now, Jackie. Fucking Al Capone was an asshole who let the Feds trick him and he deserved what he got. Now...what I have to tell you is very serious and you have to give me all your attention." He moved to stand behind his desk and opened one of the drawers, taking a paper from it. "See this paper, Jackie? It's about a man in Washington DC that has been giving us problems."

"What kind of problems? And what do I have to do with it?" She knew the answer even before Tony spoke.

"I want you to go there and get rid of him."

She had known that day would come, but didn't expect it to be so soon. She kept staring at her father and was sure her mouth was still open when he spoke again. "It has to be immediately, Jackie, he's ready to get out of the country and we have to stop him."

"But, Tony... I have never gone alone to shoot somebody. I...don't think..." she stammered, and Tony said so loud that she blinked several times. "I know all that, Jackie! But I can't trust nobody else this time. It has to be you!"

She was quick in sobering up. Crossing her father at a time like this was something that not even she dared to do. "Jeez...! Well, do you have plans for me...I mean, the written plans you have for the others?"

"Yes, they are here. You know you can change them if you need to, but try to follow all the instructions. Here's the map also, and other things you'll need." He gave her a large yellow envelope and she took it, still with trembling hands.

"Tony...are you sure you want me to do this? I've never been out alone and...what if I fuck up?"

"First of all, you have been with one of us enough times to know these things and how they work, Jackie. All I can tell you is to be tough and do as you were taught."

She gave him a weak smile. "You mean, Butt in-Tits out...?" she said remembering what he had said many times when teaching her to hold a gun with confidence.

He gave her a smirk that could have been a smile, or maybe a sign of disappointment...nobody ever knew about him. She looked at the envelope in her hands and her thoughts ran to the books she left on her bed with the assignments she was working on and the impending tests. Damn Tony, anyway!

"Tony...why can't you send someone else? Where is Marco, or Stefano?"

"They are busy right now. We have that deal going on in Georgia and I sent them both there. You have to go, Jackie – no ifs or buts!"

It was almost impossible to win a battle of wills with her father, so she just shrugged. "All right, Tony. When do you want me to leave?"

"Tomorrow will be soon enough," Thank goodness for small favors! "Go and study the papers and remember what I taught you: get the scenario in your mind and follow through. You won't fail this way."

Tony was talking to her as if she were going to go outside and drive the family car for the first time, not to end somebody's life.

"All right, Tony...and...are you paying me for this job?"

"Damn right! There will be $25,000 in your account when you get back."

Well, at least he was good at paying his bills, she knew that well.

"Sounds good, Tony. I'm going to my room and study this." She got up and left, and when she was passing by his side he took her arm. "Jackie...I know you don't want to be in the family business, but trust me this time, kid...I need you with me." She didn't say anything, but wondered about this small outburst of...what? Fatherly love? Trust in her?... Hard to tell with Tony.

With a last look into his eyes, she walked out of the room and went up the stairs and into her room. All her textbooks were on the bed as she had left them, and she marked all the pages she had been using, putting them in a neat pile on her desk. She gave out a sigh, well, this will have to wait now... as always.

Only later on she remembered that the next day was her birthday and Tony hadn't even remembered it.

She sat at the window seat and started to read the papers in the envelope. Everything was there, just as Tony had told her. A large map of the Dupont Circle area in Washington DC where the man lived, three pictures of him – a tall man with a somber face who wore a hat just like Bogey would wear in one of his movies – a picture of the front of his house, and then several papers with instructions on the man's life and daily habits. She had to know that part so her plans would not be messed up.

After two hours reading the papers and looking at the photographs, she had in mind a good profile of the man, whose name was Julius Busconi and was 45 years old.

When she was finished reading, she went to her bed to lie down. Closing her eyes, she imagined every movement she had to make to accomplish her task. She saw herself standing in front of the man's apartment, going in, maybe hiding somewhere until he got home or, if she was lucky, being invited in by him... of course, that demanded a bit more attention on her part, but as she had seen it done by others, she'd play it by ear.

She turned in bed and faced the large window. It was a rainy day in Chicago and the raindrops hit her window with force, making it almost impossible to see the front garden and lawn. She thought of many things: her mother and how much she missed her; her lonely childhood with no little friends spending the night or going to camp together; birthday parties held in the large kitchen because Tony didn't want anybody in the dining room; her first bike – a red one without training wheels because that was for sissies; her skates and how Marco and Stefano taught her to make number eights in the empty basement... seemed as if she was graduating from all that on this day. Well, if she was going to start working for Tony as an adult now, she was going to live like one. First of all, she'd get an apartment... and at this point she gave a small laugh. Yeah, right!

And Tony was going to allow it...not in a million light years! But she'll convince him, she always had before – well, always except for her schooling... - but she was confident that he'd allow her to move out. She crossed her fingers, just in case.

The next day she boarded Tony's plane at O'Hare Airport and in less than ninety minutes she was in Washington's National Airport. She knew she was on her own and with innate elegance she crossed the tarmac and went back into the airport lobby looking for the Hertz rental office. A dark sedan was available – she never reserved a car before arriving at the place – and she rented it for three days, giving her fake identity card and good credit card issued on the same fake name. Banks were crazy and would do anything for a new account, so every Tom, Dick and Harry could get a credit card these days.

The car was a medium size one, easy to drive and in a dark blue color that would blend nicely with the street traffic and would not be easily recognized. She was wearing a dark wig, pageboy style, and her green eyes were covered with brown contacts.

She looked at the map when she was sitting in the car, and started the engine, leaving the airport easily. Finding Dupont Circle, she looked for a hotel and saw the green neon lights of a Holiday Inn right by the circle. That would do, she thought. They are busy enough to recognize anyone as plain looking as me...

After checking in and going up to the fourth floor room, Jackie decided to go out and inspect the neighbourhood. She'd look touristy and would blend easily with the thousands that visit the nation's capital every day. Black trousers and a black shirt were discarded because with her dark wig she'd resemble Elvira, so she chose jeans, a red blouse and dark blue jacket. Gucci loafers without socks and a large handbag completed the outfit and she approved of her looks when she put her makeup in the large bathroom mirror.

It was almost noon when she went out. She'd stop for lunch somewhere near the man's apartment and make a mental note of everything she had learned by then. A last look at her room and she was soon out in the street, turning left towards Q Street where she knew the man lived.

It was easy to find his house. It was one of those incredible looking brownstones like the ones in New York City, obviously remodeled. The mahogany front door had panels of etched glass that probably cost thousands of dollars, and a bay window right next to it on its right; the second floor had two windows and it even had a small garret window on the third floor. She walked slowly as if looking for an address, and then, two houses down, she noticed a large red sign from a real estate office. For lease or sale, the sign read, and that gave her an idea.

She walked fast to the corner and saw three telephone booths together, and going into one of them she called the real estate office. A chirpy voice answered as 'Parsons Real Estate, how many I direct your call?' and Jackie asked to speak with one of the agents in charge of the house on Q Street.

"Wait a sec, please…" said Chirpy Voice, and she was soon connected to a man.

"I'm on the corner of Q Street and 17th," said Jackie looking at the street sign by the booth, "and I'm very interested in taking a look at a building you have for sale here."

"Are you looking at a lease or to purchase?" asked the man.

"To purchase, of course…" she said and rolled her eyes.

"All right then, I'm about five minutes from there? Can you wait in front of the house? I'll be there in a jiffy…?" His voice was effeminate and his making every sentence like a question make him sound even more so.

"Yes, fine, I'll wait there," she said and added a fast thanks but he had already left the line. Jeez, Louise! You are an eager beaver, aren't you?

But business is business and one has to do what one has to do to grab it. Jackie went back to the house and stood by the garden rail and exactly five minutes later she saw a small white Toyota Corolla stopping in front of the house. The man who got out was small and energetic, and gave her a bright smile when he saw her. "Hi there! You must be the lady who's interested in this beauty."

Jackie smiled at him and shook his extended hand. "Yes, I just moved to Washington and am looking for a place with personality, and this has lots of it."

"Oh, indeed..." he said and took a key from his pocket. "Let's go inside and you'll see how much." The door opened and he let her go first amidst a flourished wave of his arm, and he followed.

The house was undeniably beautiful inside, and Jackie wished she could really move in. Although she had only one question in mind, she still listened to everything the man said and was truly enchanted with what she saw. When they were in the kitchen, she looked out of the window. "Is there a garden also?" she asked him

"Oh yes!, come on, let's go out...All of these houses have this common garden in the back, although they are separated by this low fence."

She moved to the side of the house closer to her victim's place, and saw that he had a small glass table covered with a large umbrella, and three chairs. There were some potted plants and no house for Fido – that was good news – and the back door had glass panes.

"This is a very safe neighbourhood?," said the man, "and all the people around here have been in their house for quite some time? We always gather that type of information when we have a property in the market because buyers like to know this time of thing?" She wished he didn't speak like that, but those were things that go with the job and she had to close her ears and tolerate it.

She made some more comments and they went back to the kitchen. She leaned on the counter and he by the sink, and she continued to ask him questions. "Oh…" he suddenly said, " Silly me, I left my notebook in the car? Wait here for me for a sec, please?…and feel free to look around," and if he had known who she was he wouldn't had left the key on the counter. She quickly took a small box from her handbag, opened it, and made an impression of it. Nice. She put the key back just as the agent was coming back in the house. He gave her his card, a flyer showing all the amenities of the house and its price…high, she could see…and then beamed at her. "So, if you want to come back and take a second look just give me a jingle. What do you think so far…?"

"I really like it," she said truthfully. "It's an incredible place! But I have another appointment this afternoon that I have to keep, so I'll be in touch with you in the evening."

"All right," he said and guided her towards the front door.

Jackie thanked him again and walked fast towards the corner of 17th Street, where she turned left. All right, now she had to find a locksmith but one that would not question the impression she had made in her little box with putty. She knew, from reading Margaret Truman's detective stories, that if she went up 16th Street in the direction away from the White House, she'd find a rather seedy neighbourhood, so she turned around and crossed the street at the corner going east, she figured, towards 16th Street. When she got to that corner she turned left and walked about five blocks in an area that got worse as she continued. Stores were small and with men loitering in front, there were more bars, and she even saw a couple of women that were obviously prostitutes standing by the curve. She finally saw a small market with the sign We Make Keys While U Wait on the window and went in. A black young man smiled at her. "How you doin' hon?" he said, looking her over.

She smiled back and put her hand into her handbag where her gun was. "Well, first of all, I'm not your hon… and second, I need a key made."

He was a bit surprised and took a step back although his toothless smile didn't leave his ugly face. "Well, don't take it so seriously…You can't blame a man for trying…"

"Trying what?" she asked and gave him the coldest look this side of the Mississippi.

He shook his head. "Nothin… Forget it… Did you say you need a key made?"

She took the little box and gave it to him. "Copy this, please…"

He took it and looked at it closely. "Mmmm… Haven't seen one of these doo-hinkies for a loooong time…Is this a legal key?"

She looked around the place. "As if you cared! Just make the key and tell me how much I owe you."

Somehow her assertive manner got to him and he shrugged, moving to his right to a machine that was covered with a plastic Glad bag. In less than ten minutes Jackie had a key made and, having been trained by her cousin Stefan in those things, she placed the key to the putty. It was a good job, she had to admit, but then, the man probably made 90% of his living copying assorted keys. "How much is it?" she asked him.

"$7.50 for you…" he said and gave her the toothless smile again.

"Right. And for the rest is $5.00, right…?"

It took him a minute to realize what she had said. "Ha-ha! Pretty and a sense of humor too…"

She threw a ten-dollar bill on the counter and walked out, leaving him looking at the bill against the light from the window.

No more walking in this place, she thought, I'll probably catch lice or something worse! And stood in the corner waiting to see a taxi. One came a moment later and she went into it, giving the address of the hotel in Dupont Circle.

According to her notes, the man worked for the Department of Immigration and Naturalization Services and had been moving papers around to accept certain people into the country that had no business being here. He was in Tony's payroll but was getting greedy and had asked Tony for a large amount instead of the smaller ones he received every time he did something for the Quaglia organization. Tony's spies soon found out that the man was planning to leave the country and of course, that triggered (no pun intended) Tony's decision about stopping him. He got home around six every day, and usually had dinner alone or went to one of the many restaurants in that area.

As she had the key made for the house next to him, she planned on going into his house through the back door, crossing over the low garden fence. That evening she came back to Q Street and walked slowly along the sidewalk across from the man's house and at six-ten she saw him emerging from a taxi and going into his house. She soon saw a light in the bay window, and another upstairs; she'd give him a few more minutes to see if he was going out or staying in. Her waiting was long because at around seven-thirty she saw him leaving the house again and walked towards his right. Maybe he was going to a restaurant. She followed him and indeed saw him entering one of the restaurants in the block o 17th Street between Q and P Streets, and in a few more minutes she saw him being ushered by a waiter to one of the tables in the middle of the dining room. Good enough. She turned around and walked fast towards the empty house. The new key worked beautifully and she went into the long hallway towards the kitchen and the door that led to the garden. Standing in the shadows, she looked at the house between this and the man's but didn't see any lights, so she climbed the fence easily, run the few yards to the other fence which she climbed again, and saw herself in the man's garden. She looked around again and approached the back door that had a gorgeous glass that belonged probably in one of the windows of Notre Dame Cathedral in Paris. Although in the back of her mind she hated to break the glass, she took a rubber sphere from her handbag and placed against the glass, and pressing on it, she felt the diamond-edged blade touch the window. She twisted the rubber sphere a bit to the left and then to the right and soon felt the piece of glass being loosened. Pulling out the rubber sphere with the glass stuck to it, she put it all in her large handbag and put her hand inside of the hole she made. The door opened easily and she went in.

She was glad there were no yapping little poodles or Pomeranians – or worse…Chihuahuas – in the house because they can certainly ruin somebody's job. In less than three minutes she walked all over the house and saw that there was a sitting room with a TV set in one corner. That room had a window to the back garden. A leather recliner was in front of the TV and because there was a TV Guide and channel changer on a low table, she figured that the man was a TV watcher. He'll probably come home from dinner and sit to watch the news before going to bed, so, there's where she was going to get to him.

The window was as tall as the ceiling, with dark curtains on the sides, and on the right of it there was an enormous mahogany piece of furniture with books and some objects d'art on the shelves. There was a narrow space between it and the window and that's where she hid. Now to wait. To pass the time, she started to recite the lesson she had been working on when Tony told her to leave Chicago, and she was happy to see that she knew it pretty well.

About one hour passed and she heard the front door opening. She heard the man come in and go straight into the kitchen. Noise of a bottle being taken out of some cupboard, a glass to follow, and ice being put into it, then liquid being poured into the glass and his steps towards the sitting room where she was hiding.

She saw him when he entered the room although he never even looked to where she was. He took the TV changer and put on the ABC channel, then moved the pillow in the chair and sat down. When he took his first sip, Jackie came out from behind the curtain and faced him. He was so surprised that his drink spilled a bit on his shirt.

"Who the hell are you, and how did you come in?" he asked her.

"Are you Julius Busconi?"

"Who the hell are you?" He tried to get up but she moved her gun a bit higher, right in front of his face.

"Temper, temper…are you Busconi?"

"Yes, I am Busconi. Now tell me who you are."

"I was sent by the Quaglia organization… does that answer your question?"

He was quiet for just a moment, and then said, "You have the wrong man. I'm not the man..." and suddenly realized that he was going to say something stupid and shut up.

"Yes, I believe you are the man I wanted to see. The one who is trying to get more money from the organization...I have news for you, asshole, you are not getting any." She then aimed at his forehead and shot once. His drink spilled all over his shirt and pants, and the hand with the TV changer fell on the side of the chair.

Jackie looked at him for a moment, put the gun in her handbag and took a last look at the room seeing that nothing had been disturbed. She walked towards the kitchen and seeing the bottle still on the counter, she took a drying towel from a hook on the wall, she used it to handle the bottle. She filled a paper cup from a Mountain Spring bottle water machine and drank it. The drink, it was whisky, burned her throat and esophagus and she shook her head, then, putting the paper container in her handbag, left the kitchen through the back door making sure it was well locked.

She went fast through the next-door yard then went into the empty house again, and in less than two minutes she was out of it walking towards the hotel at a regular pace.

When she got there, she looked behind her casually but saw no one and, entering the hotel lobby she climbed the stairs to the fourth floor because she felt too hyper to wait for the elevator.

She dropped her handbag on the floor and ran to the telephone. Tony answered the call on the second ring. "Tony!," she said in a hiss, "get me out of here."

"Whatssematta Jackie? You OK?"

"Yes, I am fine. Everything went well, but get me out of this town!"

"OK, the plane will be waiting for you at 10 AM. Can you make it by then?"

"Of course I can! See you tomorrow." She was shaking when she put the receiver down and just stood there holding herself tightly. She wasn't a sissy like Tony usually said – albeit knowing she wasn't! – but she had never killed anyone and this first time had been not only exhausting but also depressing. Why did she come to DC? Why didn't she stand strong and told Tony to go fuck himself? Why…why… why?

The feeling didn't pass although she got into a tub full of hot water and tried to shrink her smooth skin with it, and she got out of the water feeling as badly as she had felt before she went into it.

The next morning, very early, she got up and went for a long run along Embassy Row and when she was tired and hungry she came back to the hotel. A breakfast of strong coffee and French toast filled her stomach, and at 9:15 she was checking out of the hotel and in a taxi towards National Airport. She didn't trust herself driving the rented car. Tony's jet was there as promised and she got into it without saying much to the pilot and co-pilot who were watching her with concern in their eyes.

She was in Tony's office two hours later, giving him an account of what had happened. "And I did it a day before because the opportunity presented itself. I was going to watch his movements one more day, but even the night was right – no moon and a bit rainy."

Tony chewed on his cigar. "Yeah...well, 'all is well that ends well', as they say in Alabama," he said and chuckled.

"Shakespeare said that, Tony..." she said in a low voice.

"Whateva...Anyway, Jackie, you did good and I'm proud of you. Ah! And I did put the money in your account, so you are a few bucks richer today."

Was this a good time to tell him that she wanted to move to her own place? "Tony... I wanted to say something now that we are in that subject..."

"What? You not happy with what I pay you?"

"No, it's fine...but I wanted to tell you that I want to invest my money in real estate and get an apartment or townhouse somewhere..."

"Why? What's wrong with the house where you were born?"

"Nothing is wrong with this house, Tony... but I turned twenty-one and I want to do it."

To her surprise, he sat down and said. "Well, tell you what... Genaro Martinelli has that building on Lake Shore Drive and is trying to sell it. If you like it I can speak to him and you not only get one hell of a place but also a great investment..."

She couldn't believe it! "The one that is at least nine floors? Tony! Would you really speak with him?"

"Sure. He's coming to see me tomorrow at noon. Join us for lunch and we can talk him out of it easily."

She didn't like the way that sounded and asked, "What do you mean by that?"

"He's strapped, Jackie. That whore he married went home to France and took everything. He's almost broke and told me that the building has to go."

From that moment on, Jackie and Tony had become a bit closer and he helped her purchase the building. She moved in as soon as it was possible, and life went on with big changes for Jackie. Tony started to trust her more and more with hits outside of Chicago and she became the best, better than Marco y Stefano and all the others. They knew it and accepted it because the money they were earning didn't allow them to complain, and besides, they knew that Jackie would dare to do anything that was put in front of her. That was the reason why she was the best.

Her only problem was the Rossi family, and she knew deep inside that she'd take care of them one day – a day probably not too far away.

The ring of the telephone brought her back to the present time, but she didn't bother to get out to answer it. It was the line she had for Tony and whoever was giving her instructions for the hit and knew that if she answered it there would be an argument and she wasn't in the mood.

After half an hour she got out of the tub, wrapping herself luxuriously in a fluffy red towel. She was carrying her empty glass to the kitchen when the telephone rang again.

Damn you, Tony! Jackie wanted to unplug the telephone from the wall, but after a moment of continuous ringing, she plugged it in again and lifted the receiver. "Damn, Tony! What do you want?"

"Is that the way you talk to your father?"

"No, it isn't. I should have said 'what the fuck do you want?' but because you are my father, I controlled myself."

"Jackie, you have too much sarcasm in you, and that ain't good. Now… how did it go in Boston?"

Jackie sighed. "It went well, how else? I waited for him in front of the warehouse, and when he was out in the sidewalk, I killed him."

"Good. That's very good, Jackie", Tony made a small pause. "Now, there's another job ready for you, this time in New Orleans…" but she interrupted him.

"New-fucking-Orleans? Tony, it's August, there must be three hundred degrees in New Orleans, plus the humidity. Do you want to kill me?"

Tony's voice was slow but ominous. "Jackie…lissen to me, Jackie… You are the only person who can do this job."

"Oh, BS Tony! Since when I'm the only person available? What about Vittorio, or Carlo, or you, for Pete's sake! I just came back today after three days of stalking that guy and you want to send me out again? It's not fair!"

"Life ain't fair, Jackie. Rest today, and tomorrow afternoon Dino will pick you up to take you to the airport."

She let out a big sigh and then asked him, "OK, what is it this time?"

"There's a man in New Orleans" he pronounced it 'Orleens', "that has done something bad for our organization. He's a lawyer with the D.A.'s office down there…"

"The D.A.'s office?" Jackie interrupted him.

"Don't interrupt your father, Jackie. Yes, the D.A.'s office. What? D'you think that because they work for the damn D.A. they don't do nothing bad?"

She sighed and looked at the ceiling. "Go on, Tony..."

"OK. This man is the one in charge of prosecuting Vito Vanieri and Mark Pollietto... you know, the drug bust that went bad for us. We are sure that he's going to send them to the clink for many moons."

"And what do we gain by getting rid of him? They'll put another lawyer on the case as soon as he is interred."

"Exactly. And that will give us time to send Vanieri and Pollietto into hiding." He made a pause and then continued slowly. "Jackie, this lawyer is the same who sent cousin Stefano up the river two years ago."

Stefano was Jackie's favorite cousin. Both of the same age, Stefano had come to the Big House to live when his parents were killed, and he and Jackie became like brother and sister. When he was caught and tried in Louisiana, Jackie had been there with him and swore to him that she'll seek revenge one way or another.

"I see..." was her response. She looked up at the ceiling as if waiting for an answer to be engraved there. Damn Tony always knew what buttons to push. "When am I supposed to leave?"

"Like I said, tomorrow afternoon. Dino will take you to the airport and the jet will be ready for you at about 1 PM. Rest today, get things ready tomorrow. I'll send you the usual papers by fax in a moment." he was silent for a moment. "Jackie, I'm getting old and you know I want you to be the head of our organization..."

"Yeah, right, Tony... We have discussed this until we were both blue in the face. You know damn well that the rest of them are not going to accept me..."

"Jackie... They all know you have the brains here. They're almost there, trust me. Every time we meet I mention you and the things you have done for us. You are the only person who hasn't been caught, or arrested, or nothing... All your hits have been works of art and they know it."

"What about the Rossis?"

"Well... the Rossis are a different chapter. There are two boys there and they both think they should have the job, but they are too well known by the police even if nothing has been proved. They are stupid, and one of these days they are going to end up in the clink. That's why I want you. They don't like the idea that there's a woman involved – they don't want to believe it either. Anyway, Jackie... I'll send you the paperwork and you be ready tomorrow."

"OK, Tony, but when I get back we have to talk... serious talk!"

"That's OK, babe. We'll do that." And he disconnected the call. Jackie stood by her desk, telephone in hand thinking that for sure her father had already forgotten the conversation they had just had.

She walked slowly to her bedroom, threw away the red towel and got into bed naked. She heard the fax machine humming a few minutes later but didn't get up to see what Tony was sending her. She'll deal with it tomorrow in the morning.

A very hot and sunny day greeted Jackie when she woke up the next day. She showered and went to the kitchen to make coffee and while it was brewing, she went to her office and gathered all the papers that Tony had faxed the evening before. She read them while sipping her coffee within the coolness of her kitchen.

The man, Otis Lieberman, was 44 years old and had been with the D.A.'s office for seven. He lived alone on the fifth floor of an apartment building in the center of New Orleans, had a girlfriend of sorts from Baton Rouge, who worked in New Orleans, and family in Florida.

Jackie studied the plan of the apartment and read the information about the man's daily movements. Thank goodness he was one of those men who does the same things every day – another bore – and following his life should not be very difficult. She would take her short barrel gun for this job. Her mind had already made a plan and hoped she'd be able to follow it. Sometimes things happen during the job and plans had to be changed. Those changes had put her life in danger more than once, like the time in Ohio when the victim's lover had come out of the bedroom stark naked, and she had to kill her as well.

Jackie sat down to study the papers, made a plan that she read several times to learn it well, and a couple of hours later she burned all those notes in the large fireplace she had in the living room.

At eleven she called Tony. "Hello Jackie, did you sleep well?"

"Yes, Tony, thanks... OK, tell me more about this man." She didn't have to say anything else. Tony understood.

"Everything is in the papers I faxed to you, Jackie. He's set on getting a conviction, no matter what. As soon as he's taken care of we are sending the boys into hiding."

"Are they out right now?"

"No, of course not. They are being kept in a small county jail in a godforsaken cow town in Louisiana, a few miles from New Orleans. They come and go to Court whenever they have to, but as soon as this creep is gone we are gonna stop the van that transports them and get them out."

"What makes you think you are going to be successful?"

"Aren't we always? The van has just the driver in it, plus the prisoners. It's gonna be stopped a few miles out of the small town and that's it."

"I don't know how you do it, Tony."

He gave a small laugh. "Emilio has been studying the way they do it. We know even in which pocket the driver keeps the keys. Anyway, Jackie... you just take care of that lawyer and we'll do the rest."

How was she going to talk to her father and tell him she was quitting? She sighed. It wasn't going to be easy, she knew it, but for her own peace of mind, she'd have to do it.

When Tony forbade her to go to university, Jackie had searched colleges that would give degrees by correspondence, and when she found one she enrolled, obtaining her degree in less than the allotted four years. Tony never knew about this. If she could hide that from him, she could also hide herself. She had the fake IDs and money to support herself for the rest of her life. She had opened an account in Zurich and had enough to live in luxury for the rest of her life – and away from her 'family', she hoped. Tony continued, "There's a bonus for you with this one, Jackie. That is because I'm asking you to do another job so close to the last one."

"OK, sounds good. And, Tony...? Please, don't give me another job right now. I have something else to do."

"Like what? What d'you mean 'you got somethin' to do?"

"I have a private life too, Tony. I want to do something for myself, and by myself..."

There was a silence on the other end of the line and Jackie knew her father was not a happy camper. "Is there a man somewhere, Jackie?" He finally said, his voice ominous.

She gave a short laugh. "There are men everywhere, Tony..."

"Jackie, quit the sarcasm and the shit. You know what I mean."

"Yes, Tony, I know. But there's no man in my life, dammit, but what if there were? What are you going to do about it?"

"For one thing, see that he's worthy of you. If he was, I'd welcome him to the Quaglias."

She laughed, hard this time. "Yeah, right! Imagine me, married... Then, when the little ones came, I can say to them, 'darling, I'm sorry mommy can't go watch your first game because I have to go to Atlanta to kill somebody...'... No, thank you, Tony. I'd never put a child through the same shit I went through. Look, forget this conversation, all right? I have to get ready to go to the airport. Is the limo coming for me?"

"Jackie, you have been acting funny lately. What's going on? You have never been a rebel, and now, every time I talk to you, you have some new issue up your ass."

"Tony... let's leave it, OK?"

"I don't want to leave it! You talk to me now!"

Jackie let out a sigh. "All right, if you want to discuss it now, we will. What was trying to tell you at the beginning of this conversation was that I need some time, some free time, for myself. I want to get things into perspective."

She'll get it done, for sure, and then, after she got back to Chicago, she'll sit with her father and tell him she had something else to do.

"Like what? What d'you mean 'you got somethin' to do?"

"I have a private life too, Tony. I want to do something for myself; alone...I want to see new places. I want to meet new people, someone who doesn't know who I am and what I do. I just want to have a relaxed vacation without the thought of having to hide or to disguise myself because if I don't, my life could be in danger. That's what I want, Tony. I am twenty-seven years old, and all I've done in the last ten is... this... Do you realize that I don't have even one friend my age? Never had, for that matter…"

"Is that what's botherin' you? That's easy to fix, Jackie. When you get back from New Orleans you can take the time you need. And you know somethin'? It's gonna be on my account. You make the arrangements and I'll pay for whatever it is. How's that?"

Jackie shook her head and looked at the ceiling. Why talking to Tony if everything he says translates to money? He'd never understand her needs, in a million years. Taking a look at her watch, he said, "All right, Tony. I'll do just that. Send the car, please. I'll be ready as soon as it gets here."

With a deep sigh, she looked around her beautiful room and thought why having all these riches if she was never home to enjoy them. Walking towards the stereo, she chose Elvis' Greatest Hits and walked to her room to get a small suitcase ready for her trip. She had an idea how she was going to do this hit and chose the clothes she'd need. The King's voice followed her all over the apartment, and she walked following the music rhythm of each catchy tune.

"Yes, darling Elvis, you said it: it's now or never…" A wide smile shone on her face.

CHAPTER THREE

Tony's limo was on time, as always, and navigated the busy streets of Chicago with ease. Vinnie hadn't come this time and she sat alone in the spacious back seat and she thought about her life again, her futile, fruitless, ineffective life. Oh, yes. As soon as she got back from this last trip she'd sit with Tony and will make him understand that she was getting out.

She closed her eyes. Who was she kidding beside herself? Tony will ignore her words, as always, and she'd go back to her showcase of an apartment and keep planning the hits just as she had been doing until now. Bloody fucking life!

When they got to the airport, Dino turned around from his front seat and smiled at Jackie. "Here we are, Signorina. Anything else?"

She gave him the smile she knew he was waiting for. "No, Dino, gratzie. Thanks for the ride..."

"No, Signorina Jackie, thanks to you. You bring the sun to the strongest storms." His English was accented and he always translated directly from Italian, but his words always left Jackie elated. Jesus! The kid could easily be her kid brother!

He got out of the car and came around to open Jackie's door, took her small carrying case, and started to walk towards the plane that was waiting just fifty yards from the car, but Jackie took the case from him and dismissed him with her hand, then she got on her toes and kissed his cheek. He beamed. "I'll be back in about four days, Dino, so I'll see you then. I'll take this." The young man hesitated for a moment, but gave her the case not sure he had done the right thing. He stood there by the car, watching Jackie walk towards the waiting jet, and didn't move until she climbed the stairs and turned around to wave good-bye.

Once in the luxurious aircraft, Jackie greeted Rick Milano and the American co-pilot and sat in her favorite chair, accepting immediately a cool drink from another young man whom she knew from other flights. One thing for sure, Tony knew how to surround himself with comfort and opulence, and he wasn't a miser with his minions either. Oh, well, she thought with a sigh, I won't miss this splendor. I have enough to do the same by myself. Well... almost enough! She chuckled as she fastened her seatbelt, ready for yet another journey into the unknown.

The jet landed in a smaller airport not far from New Orleans, and Jackie – after making arrangements with Rick Milano for her pick up, walked towards the Hertz office. There was no car waiting because she, for security reasons, never made reservations in advance. She preferred to get there and rent whatever was available at the time.

The less paper trail she left, the better and more secure her business would be.

The woman behind the Hertz counter was as black as a real African, her skin was almost blue, and Jackie thought that she was indeed beautiful. She chose a dark blue full-size car and said she'd bring it back in one week. Another false trail.

"Are you planning to leave the State, Miss Collins, and, are you going to be the only driver?" The woman asked the question without looking up from the computer screen. Good. Jackie's large sunglasses covered a good portion of her face.

"Yes, I'll stay here in the city, and I'll be the only driver, thank you."

When the tedious paperwork was done, Jackie signed the three forms, picked up her fake license and good credit cards made out to the false name on the license, and, dropping everything in her large purse, gave the woman a small smile and left the office. Somebody had brought the car right to the door and she got in, after giving the kid that drove it five dollars. Tony's voice came to her head, "… and never leave too large tips. People remember others that way."

Driving into New Orleans, she went over the plan she had; her meticulous mind covering every step she'd take until she had to face her target. The heat of the day was worse than that of Boston a few days ago, and when she saw the sign for a Sleep Inn she decided to stop. A cool room and a long cold shower were what she needed right now, and that hotel chain was usually good enough for her.

Just as she thought, the lobby was busy and she was able to secure a room for three nights – she'd check out the same day of the hit. The older man who made the room reservation didn't bother to ask for extra identification when she wrote her assumed name, Carla Collins, of Cedar Rapids, Iowa, and wrote a fake business address and name of company.

The man, however, looked at the business name. "Fancy that," he said, "I have a brother-in-law that works for Amana too... Small world!"

"It's a very large company and yes, a very small world..." small enough for you to remember me... Her smile was genuine and she hoped the man would not ask her any more questions.

"Have a good stay in New Orleans, Miss Collins."

"Thank you... Ralph," she answered, reading the name on the man's nametag. Taking her keys, she walked fast towards the second floor where her room was. "Damn! Imagine that... someone who may remember me... I wonder if I should change motels..." But she kept walking at the same pace, not giving away any worries.

The room was quite nice, with a view of the city and the large Louisiana Superdome to her left, a building that looked at if some god had dropped a dish from the heavens and it had fallen upside down in the middle of the city. Tony supplied her with the latest maps and city information every time she had to travel "on business", and she opened the map on her queen-size bed and started to study it.

The exact address was also given, but because people do move sometimes at the spur of the moment, Jackie preferred to always double-check that information in person to make sure he was not shooting someone else. Ha!, that would be something else, she thought.

Let's see... she mumbled, I'm right here. If I take this freeway to Tulane Street and follow it this way... yeah, I want to study the criminal court where he works, and then I have to follow him home. Now... he's a single man, so, chances are he lives close to his office... I wonder if he walks to work. I don't dare to hire a cab and ask him to follow him home because that would be the biggest mistake I've ever made... so, I have to hope and pray that... She stopped her musing for a moment, and then she reached towards the large telephone book by the bed. Jackie... Hello? What the fuck are telephone books for? Wake up! The phone book was a brand new one, and by looking at the man's name, she saw that everything given to her by Tony was still valid.

The attorney's name was in the telephone book with two addresses, one of them right by the courts building, so she figured that was the office. The other address was on Royal Street – his apartment or house. Going back to her fancy city map, she found that Royal Street passes Lafayette Square. Duh! She mumbled again, maybe that's why his building is called The Lafayette Manor... He's close to that Square. All right, this is good! I'm going to locate his house today, but first, a nice long bath and a telephone call. Her Cheshire Cat smile shone when she walked towards the shower.

CHAPTER FOUR

The water in the tub was hot in spite of the temperature outside, but hot water was the best to relax, and Jackie wanted to let all her worries to go down the drain; she wanted a clear mind and, dammit! Tony was not going to interfere. She undressed and got into the tub where the bubbles from an expensive bath oil bottle were welcoming her. Her eyes closed and she cleaned her mind from all kinds of thoughts.

She had never had an easy life. Her sheltered life changed abruptly when her mother died a month after Jackie turned seventeen and her father had called her into his office to have what he called "a manly talk".

Jackie, from that moment on, had realized that she was not going to lead a normal life, go to college as she wanted, and maybe in the future own her own business – anything that would separate her from the kind of life her father wanted her to lead.

Tony had been adamant: she would join the 'family' business; she'd be trained and taught by the best – he had said – and would take his place when the time came. Jackie had pleaded, supplicated, and appealed to her mother's wishes of a normal life for her only daughter, but Tony was nothing but a stubborn son-of-a-bitch. His wish had to be done, as it had always been, and Jackie was at the time, too distraught about her mother's death to argue with him. She figured that her obstinate father would change his mind when she proved to be an unteachable dummy, but she was wrong. Blessed with a brilliant mind, she had shown her father – albeit against her own will – that she would be an asset to the Quaglia organization. So she stayed, always waiting for the right time to get out. Yeah, right!

Another hit by herself when she was twenty-one had proved she could do it. Of course, she had broken her ankle that day, but, hey! Accidents happen, don't they? She had been inside the house of a well-known senator in Michigan when she heard the front door open. Looking around for shelter, she saw a window and make a run towards it, but unfortunately, the window was on a higher level of the garden outside, and the ground was at least three feet lower than she figured. She landed on her left leg and felt an acute pain in her ankle. She remembered the pain she had felt when she broke her leg when she was twelve and it was the same. The pain shot all the way up her leg and she sat on the wet ground among rose bushes that, adding insult to intense injury, pricked her arms and hands making her wish she could scream her head off.

The senator had got his, though. When she realized he was alone in the room, she just placed her pistol aimed with a silencer on the windowsill and shot him in the head, just the way she had been told. Then she got the hell out of there.

Tony had been livid with anger when she told him what happened. "Dammit, Jackie," he had shouted, "How can you take that risk! Shooting the man from the outside of the house! What if somebody saw you? Don't you know those guys sometimes have secret service men with them? What the hell is the matter with you?"

Only four hours later he had come to her room and asked her how her ankle was. The book she threw at him from the window seat where she was resting, told him what her daughter thought of him.

Yes, that was Tony. And yet, she had never doubted he loved her. There was something in his personality; in the way he spoke to her either when teaching her a new trick or just asking for her company in his overbearing office, that told her that he was proud of her. But then, he didn't have a son so she would have to do.

Tony was an enigma, a puzzle that Jackie, with her brilliant mind, wanted to decipher but felt she never could or would. What man puts his only child in such danger, sometimes three, four times a month? What man would train his child to kill without sorrow? Was that love? Was that an excuse to claim he wanted his 'family' to have a strong leader when he was gone? What exactly was Tony Quaglia? Jackie had spoken to one of her Psychology teachers once and told him that she wanted to write fiction one day and had an idea in mind, but needed his input. The man had given her a most disturbing account of personality disorders that matched her father's, and Jackie added 'fear' to the many other feelings she had for Tony. She wanted to please him, didn't take his insults too personally, and learned to ignore his outbursts – but deep inside she knew that he was one of the most dangerous men she would ever encounter. Whether he'd ever hurt her she didn't know – didn't dare to ask herself – but she was sure that he'd take very serious steps if she'd ever failed him.

Because of her way of life, Jackie didn't dare to have a personal relationship with anyone. She was having an affair with life at this moment and anything else would be stepping on too many people's toes, and what was worse, putting the life of that person in danger. Besides, she didn't want to have relationships with any of the men she met in her daily life. That's why she had an America On Line account and used her available screen names to meet people in the Internet.

She had met PuppyDoc one day while she surfed the chat rooms, and found a conversation about careers – one of the few serious chats she had ever been into. She had come into the chat room and just sat there, observing the chatters, then suddenly an Instant Message had popped up asking her why she was just "sitting there" without taking part. She had answered that she had been "listening" and waiting for a chance to give an opinion. They started to talk and after two hours made an appointment for the next day – and that's the way she had met him. There was no personal information exchanged – her rule – only conversation about many different matters. He had insisted on sending his photo and she was pleasantly surprised to see that he was about thirty or thirty-two, with piercing blue eyes and dark hair, and extremely good looking. He also lived in Ireland, in a small fishing village called Tralee Bay right in the famous Ring of Kerry and near the town of Tralee. That was safe enough, she thought at the time, but what if he actually lived in Arkansas and was lying through his teeth? After all, that's what she was doing, and lying in the Internet was a way of life to millions these days. She'd had to go slowly and try to pry as much as she could out of him.

The chance to find out came about two months later when he had asked her for her telephone number. No way, she had said, you have to understand that I cannot do that... but if you want to give me yours I'll call you. Apparently he had no problems doing that and gave it to her – both his home and office numbers, so she called him. He sounded wonderful, with a soft Irish lilt in his very well educated English. Jackie was elated to have found someone like him – his name was Aidan Cassidy – and he was a vet - the only and beloved, he explained – in his area.

She knew it was crazy, but couldn't help herself. She really hated to lie to this wonderful man who seemed to be so down to earth and 'normal', but there's no way she could tell him – or anybody else – her real story, so she made up something that had a lot of truth but none of the many details her real life was so full of. They had been sending e-mails and chatting on the telephone for almost five months now, and Aidan had asked her to please give him her telephone so he could call her. Having lots of extra money to spend had some advantages, and one of them was to get anything she wanted, so another telephone line in her apartment was put just for her and Aidan's use. The line was very private, with no directory information tied to it, so, if Aidan one day decided to inquire about where she lived, there would be no address showing. She had also been using calling cards to call him when she was not at home, her trained mind having covered all the possibilities of being found out. She had told Aidan that she worked for her father – true – and that she traveled extensively in her job – true – contacting people that were in business with Tony – half true. Jackie hoped that Aidan would never even fathom her real life, and since he appeared in her life, she had been more than careful in planning and carrying out her work. One mistake and she'd be caught, and that meant losing her freedom and losing Aidan forever.

One day, a few years back, she and Tony were planning a hit in which she felt very unsafe because of the situation and because it was in Mexico – a country that lock people up first and ask questions afterwards. Tony had told her that if anything went wrong he already had a back-up plan in which Jackie would appear to have been framed up by someone else – someone from one of the other 'families'. Jackie trusted her father about keeping her protected, and hoped before every hit, that he'd have a plan standing by.

After getting to know the Quaglia organization, Jackie was amazed at how its wheels went around and how well organized everything was. She did trust Tony, but wished his views were not so closed, and that thought kept her awake more than one night. When the time came and she'd told Tony that she was getting out, everything should fit into place so that Tony would not make her impossible to leave. The problem was, how would she accomplish that?

Jackie felt the water becoming colder and colder and the bubbles disappear until there was only a thin layer of whitish soap on the surface of the tub. She got out and dried herself quickly, wrapped herself in the large towel and walked to the bedroom where she sat on the bed and reached for the telephone. She was using one of her calling cards and it took a moment for the operator to connect the call to a sleepy village in Ireland. She heard the already familiar double rings but there was no answer. She then tried Aidan's office thinking that perhaps he was working late, and again found nobody. Leaving the telephone on its cradle, she tried to hide her disappointment and started to dress, ready to go out and figure the best way to get into the attorney's apartment and kill him.

Damn this life, anyway!

CHAPTER FIVE

Following the street maps she had gathered, Jackie took Interstate 10 and the exit to Tulane Avenue and soon found the Criminal-Court Magistrate building, where she knew Otis Lieberman worked. She parked the car in a 30-minute parking space she found and studied the area, mostly, she looked for a bar or pub nearby, knowing that the attorney visited one after work almost every day. There were some, and she was glad to see that they were all within walking distance from the Courts. Written notes were not her forte because she knew never to leave a paper trail, so her mind had been accustomed to taking everything in.

Next was to find his apartment house. Lafayette Square was one of the many grassy squares that fill New Orleans neighborhoods, and the fact that this one had benches under its many trees made things easier for Jackie. She parked the car on one of the side streets of the square, and walked the remaining block to face the apartment house where Lieberman lived. It was an eleven-story building with two apartments on each floor – both apartments separated by a high wall in the balcony. When Jackie saw the building, a wide smile crossed her face because one of the apartments in the seventh floor was empty and a large "FOR LEASE" sign had been put across the balcony. She thought for a few moments and made a decision.

Walking fast, she crossed the street and entered the building. The doorman was sitting in his cubicle, reading yesterday's evening paper and looked up when he saw her. "Evening Madam..." he said with a smile. Jackie greeted him and looked around the lobby. Marble and green palms looked back at her, and her eyes turned back to the doorman.

"I was wondering about the empty apartment on the seventh floor?"

He put the paper on the table and gave him his attention. "Yes? It just became vacant and it's being painted at this moment, but if you want to take a peek...?"

"That will be nice. What's the number?"

"710. Just take this elevator and go up. There are painters there, but you won't bother them. Tell them that I sent you..."

"And your name is...?

"Tony, at your service Madam."

Fancy that. "All right, Tony. Be right back..." and with another killer smile, she walked quickly towards the elevators. She was in the seventh floor in less than a minute and walked left to the apartment with the open front doors and the voice of some punk rapper coming from it.

The two painters didn't hear her come in, so she just took a fast look at the apartment's layout, noticing that the entrance hallway led to a large living room with a French door on the opposite wall, probably the balcony that faced the street. On the right there was a modern kitchen, and farther on through the hall, two other doors – probably bedrooms. One feature that she noticed was a large L-shaped divider right in the middle of the living room, as if it had been put there to separate the living room area from the entrance hall. Interesting, she thought, nice place to play hide 'n seek...

At that moment one of the painters turned around and saw her and he said something to his partner, who turned around and looked at her from head to toe. "Hello..." was his greeting, and if he had been wearing a tie he would have arranged it.

"Hi! Just looking around. Tony downstairs said it was OK..." She used her "cutie-pie voice".

"Oh, sure... need a guide?"

Pig! "No thanks; you carry on with your work and I'll look at the size of the rooms."

"No problem. Call if you need anything."

She didn't answer and walked towards the L-shaped thing in the living room. The inside angle of the L faced the room itself leaving a nice hiding corner. The rest of the apartment took a few more minutes to look and she was soon saying good-bye and thank you to the painters, who had stopped their work again when she left.

The outside hall only had the two doors to the only apartments in that floor, the elevator double doors, and another door at the end with a lighted sign on top showing the stairs exit.

Jackie thought about going down to the fifth floor where Lieberman's apartment was, but discarded the idea just in case the attorney was getting home and saw her loitering near his door.

Down in the lobby, Tony the doorman approached her when she left the elevator. "Well, what d'you think?"

"Seems nice. From the front, is that the right or left apartment?"

"The right one. They all look the same, and the left side ones are their mirror image. That means..." but she interrupted him.

"Yes, I know what that means. You have any idea of the rent?"

"Eighteen-hundred – but all the utilities except telephone, are included."

"Deposit?" She hoped she was asking all the right questions.

"A thousand cleaning deposit, and you have to sign a one-year lease. You interested?"

She looked around the expensive lobby. "I may be... I'm getting married in a month and we are just looking right now."

Tony took a card from his pocket and gave it to her. "Here. Take this card and if you decide to inquire, my name is on the other side. They'll know I sent you." Right. And you get a pretty commission... But that was all right; we all have to do what we have to do.

She took the card and thanked Tony, leaving the building and walking fast towards her car. That was easy enough. Now she knew that Lieberman's apartment, which was number 511, was the mirror image of 710 because it was on the other side, and her mind was already creating a scenario that would lead to the death of the attorney.

Jackie sometimes astonished herself when she contemplated her life, and this time she started to feel that same old mood she had been having regarding the way she lived. Never before had she felt the need to think twice about what she did, but these days that need was there and Jackie's loyalty to her father was being hindered by the consciousness that her work brought to her senses.

Those thoughts were going through her mind while she drove around the downtown area looking for a place to have dinner. The problem was not to find a restaurant because there were a million of them within a one-mile radius, but to find a parking space was. She finally chose a French-looking place that had a space right in front. Whatever… she decided, I can park here and that's my main concern.

The food was quite good and the Creole woman that served her seemed like the real thing and recommended an incredible Cajun catfish that left her entire mouth on fire. Jackie thought about Aidan while she ate and regretted the time change with Ireland and the fact that it was too late for her to call him. Tomorrow, first thing, she promised herself while paying the bill. She went back to the table and left a nice tip for the waitress who asked her politely if she had enjoyed the meal. "It was more than wonderful!" said Jackie, "I'll be back."

But she probably wouldn't. She could not afford to be seen in the same place twice, just in case; the chances to be recognized were too great and she could not chance it.

The drive back to the motel was uneventful, just her thoughts were still swirling around in her head, and once there, she started to plan her real strategy for the hit.

CHAPTER SIX

Jackie didn't sleep late the next day although she wanted to. The night before she had taken her yellow pad and written down the plan she had to kill Otis Lieberman. She read it many times until her own words were engraved in her mind and afterwards she took the pages to the bathroom and burned them in the toilet. No paper trails allowed.

At seven in the morning she dialed Aidan's telephone number in Ireland and chatted with him for twenty minutes, and when he asked where she was, she said Cleveland. After they finished talking she hated herself for lying to him, but once more she swore she'd tell him the truth about herself and her 'family'.

Oh, come on, Jackie Quaglia! You know damn well you'll never tell him the truth. You're a killer, and he's a healer... albeit of dogs and cats. He saves lives and you destroy them with one bullet. What a predicament, girl!

Go to hell, damn conscience!

Ten minutes after she placed the telephone receiver on its cradle, she opened her suitcase and took out a plain flowered skirt and white T-shirt; she wore sandals, dark glasses and a funky hat with a daisy up front. It was so hot already that she didn't wear make-up, just a bit of mascara and lip-gloss. She looked like a teenager ready to hit the malls as soon as they opened.

Today she was going to follow Otis Lieberman and try to figure his movements during the day. Putting his picture into her handbag, and with a last look at the room, she closed the door and left, driving straight to the area of the city where she had been the day before.

The Criminal Court-Magistrate Building was located on Tulane Avenue and she parked in a paid parking lot about two blocks from the building. She'd make herself familiar with her target by attending one of his sessions in Court. That wasn't difficult to find. The black girl that was receptionist in one of the offices told her that Attorney Lieberman was in Courtroom number 11, and Jackie followed her directions.

She sat in the last row of seats in the courtroom where her target was the prosecuting attorney in a murder case. It seemed to Jackie that it was a pretty easy case: the man charged with murdering another man for whom he used to work was as guilty as hell, and the defense attorney – a young woman so pale and colorless that she seemed to have fallen off an embalming table – was doubtless a rookie and had no chance to win her case. Not only her client had GUILTY written all over his face, but also Lieberman was giving her the ride of her life in the courtroom. The judge, an older man who looked bored to death, overruled every word she said and every time that happened, another pint of blood drained from her otherwise pretty face.

Jackie listened to everything but her eyes didn't leave Otis Lieberman. He was forty-four according to the papers Tony had given her, tall, and not at all bad looking. He probably kissed the Blarney Stone when he was very young because his words were hitting their objectives: the jury and the judge. They, as Jackie, were wrapped up in his words and their eyes followed his movements in the front of the courtroom.

Jackie left when the judge said that the case would be adjourned until that afternoon at two o'clock. She waited in the hall until Lieberman appeared at the door, holding a briefcase and looking into the pages of a daily planner, and Jackie followed him.

He walked fast towards the entrance, still looking at the planner, and greeting people here and there. Would he take a cab once outside? But he didn't. When he reached the marble steps at the front of the building, he turned right and at that moment he put away the planner, but took it out a moment later when apparently another thought hit him.

After walking slowly for a moment, he put the planner back in his pocket. She sighed and walked faster because Lieberman was entering a gray building with imposing double doors. Jackie followed him in without hesitating, and found herself in the lobby of what seemed to be the attorney's offices. She saw him head towards the elevators and saw him punch the number four. She turned around and went to the large directory that was fixed to one of the walls and, sure enough, the fourth floor alone was the prosecuting office of the District Attorney.

Well, she thought, I'm sure not going up there. Leaving the building, she walked to the corner where an almost identical copy of an English pub was located. Dark wood and brass inside, and a sign with a dark blue background and a hand lowering a gavel gave the name to the establishment. The Gavel was probably the place where all the lawyers met after work. She went in and sat at the bar; a tall man with an English accent gave her a toothy smile and asked her what she was going to have. "Do you have shandy?" she asked him in a fake but very good English accent almost better than his.

His eyebrows went up for a moment. "Not on tap like the real English one, but I carry the tinned one. Excellent too!"

"The 'Double Deck' brand?" she asked him.

"As a matter of fact, yes! I can see that you know how to drink. Where are you from?"

"Londoner." She said without hesitation.

"Oh, good. Well, here's your drink. Cheers." He took his own glass of something clear that could have been water or vodka, and finished it. It better be water.

"Cheers." She said and took a sip of the excellent shandy, her favorite drink when she visited Britain.

The man left her alone and she finished the drink, left him a forgettable tip, and walked out thanking him for the hospitality and the good wishes for a good stay in America – as he put it.

Next was to find a place to have lunch and she chose another small place that advertised the best Cajun cuisine in the city. Yeah, they all said that, but she went in and sat by the window and was soon tasting a good jambalaya and crusty French bread. That was great thing about New Orleans, any small hole on the wall had great Cajun food!

Jackie thought over her plan, and moved around in her mind the way things would work out. She was going to study Lieberman's movements that evening after work, and the next day she'd follow him home and kill him. The jambalaya didn't taste as good as it had tasted a moment ago, but she wasn't surprised. It hit her every time.

When she got back to the motel, she took out the local yellow pages and looked under Attorneys. Luckily, the DA's office had a small ad with the office working hours, and she wrote them down. After a shower, she called the office from a pay phone near the motel and asked for Otis Lieberman and, as expected, was told that he was in Court. Of course, she knew this because had heard it from the Judge that the case would adjourn until two that afternoon.

"This is Megan?," she told the secretary at the DA's office using her "cutie pie" voice with a question mark at the end of the sentence, something she disliked very much when she heard it. "I'm calling from the Governor's office? The Governor's is having a small gathering tomorrow at seven in the evening and would like Mr. Lieberman to attend."

The DA's secretary was either too impressed with the telephone call or was too used to those invitations from high places because she didn't ask any more questions, just wrote down the time and place. "I'll give Mr. Lieberman the message, Megan," she said. "Is it going to be black tie?"

"Dark business suit, please. The Governor of Maine will be present as well, and it will be cocktails and a buffet dinner. May I give you a call tomorrow to see if Mr. Lieberman will be able to attend?"

"That, or I can call you, Megan…"

Oops. "No, let me call you because I'll be working close to the Governor's staff setting up the party and you may not be able to find me. At noon is OK?"

"Oh, yes! In fact, I'll ask him this afternoon as soon as he comes back from Court, in case you want to call me back."

"Great! Thanks." Jackie left the telephone booth and walked back to the motel. Once there, she leaned back on the bed, closing her eyes for a moment.

Lieberman's secretary wrote herself a note and left it in front of her, thinking that his boss was always invited to posh places like the Governor's mansion and such, but unfortunately there was never the need to take his secretary with him. He was probably going to take that interfering, bossy attorney with her hyphenated last name and big boobs...

"Oh well," she finished, tacking down her unfinished work, "there's a big price to pay for those Governor mansion parties and Chief of Police bashes – no pun intended... Dear Mr. Lieberman is a número uno son of a bitch and his attorney friend and other henchmen can have him."

Jackie would have applauded those thoughts, but she was already planning the events of the next day. Later in the afternoon she was going to use one of her disguises and go back to the Courts, and follow Lieberman home. Attorneys are a rare breed, but a rather predictable one. The man probably did the same things day after day, and although she'd have preferred to have more days to follow him, she was certain that every day was the same for him. They have no imagination!, she thought, not knowing that she was very right.

She left the motel again at four, but before, she called the court and asked if the case that Attorney Lieberman was trying that afternoon had ended for the day. She was told that they were still in Court.

She had time to get downtown, park the car and wait outside until he left his offices.

At five she was sitting in one of the benches across from the Magistrate Building. She was lucky to find a bench in the shade of a large magnolia tree. She was a platinum blonde right now, with long straight hair and bangs, and the white skirt and aqua T-shirt and sandals made her look ten years younger. To finish the teenage appearance, she bought an ice cream from a street vendor and sat down, her eyes behind the large sunglasses not missing anything that was going on in the street.

It was almost five-thirty when she saw Lieberman leaving the Magistrate Building and walk fast towards his office, and once there, she imagined him going to the elevators, to his office, getting his messages, getting his things ready and leaving the office. She smiled to herself because a few minutes after she finished her make-believe steps, he appeared again at the door. She was again right when she saw him walking towards The Gavel, the pub at the corner.

She was tempted to go there after him, but thought better of it and remained seated, waiting for him to go home. Would he drive? She hoped not.

It was six-ten when he left again and turned back towards his office, but instead of going into, he kept walking. Yes, he was walking home – if he was going home. She waited until he was at least half a block ahead and started to follow him.

He was a fast walker, and looked at his planner once while keeping the same pace, and in less than ten minutes he entered his apartment building in Lafayette Square.

Jackie crossed the street and sat in another bench, still watching the structure, her eyes fixed on the floor where she knew his apartment was. A moment later she saw him opening the large French door that she knew was in the living room, facing the street, and he appeared there with a bottle of something in his hand. He leaned on the balcony for a long moment, sipping his drink, deep in thought. She could almost swear that at one time, his eyes met hers down there in the Square, but no, she was just another tired tourist sitting in the shade of ancient trees.

She stayed in the bench for ten more minutes, then picked up the raffia handbag she was carrying, and with a slow look at one side of the street, got up and walked slowly towards her car, a few blocks away.

It was almost nine o'clock when she got back to the motel. She had dinner in its restaurant – a sad marriage of American and French cuisines – and went back to her room where she took a long shower, watched the news, and went to sleep. Not even Aidan was in her thoughts that night, and the next morning she was up at seven, went for a long run, and came back to the motel. She was going to check out that day at noon, and then go out and look for a place where she could change her appearance.

Everything went according to her plans, and at one-thirty she left the bathroom of a fancy hotel in the downtown area. She looked so different that not even Tony would recognize her, she was sure.

She had left the motel wearing a pair of tight white jeans and red T-shirt. Her hair had been loose on her shoulders, and her large sunglasses were up on her head, ready to come down and cover her beautiful green eyes. She paid her bill with the same credit card she had shown when she checked in – a real credit card issued to a fake name.

Before she left her room, she spent almost one hour cleaning the surfaces that she knew she had touched, then, with a last look around the room, she left. An hour later she went into the parking garage of a hotel in town, about three blocks from Liberman's apartment. After checking the car, she went upstairs and into one of the rest rooms.

Leaving the hotel downtown, Jackie saw her reflection in one of the hotel large mirrors and almost smiled. She was now wearing a shoulder length wig in a brown shade, a dark blue wrap-around skirt that would turn to another color in less than a minute, a white T-shirt with tiny blue flowers, and white espadrilles. Her raffia handbag with a blonde wig inside, different sunglasses, and her .22 small revolver with silencer completed her ensemble. She mentally counted the blocks to Lafayette Square: three, and she did a last test. She walked fast to the apartment building and timed herself, seeing that she had made the trip in just nine minutes. Yes, that was all right.

She knew that her car was secure in the hotel's basement parking, and the ticket in her hand said she could be there until nine o'clock. Plenty of time to kill Lieberman, walk to the parking, get her car and get the hell out of that area towards the airport where Rick Milano would be waiting in Tony's jet.

Now she had to wait. That was always the worse part. She knew that Lieberman was going to come home directly from work because she had checked with his secretary that morning and the girl had said that yes, Mr. Lieberman would be glad to attend the cocktail party with the Governor and she was sorry he wasn't in the office at that moment, and that he expected to be in court until five that afternoon. She figured he'd come home to shower and change and that's when she'd be waiting for him in his apartment.

She sat in a bench in the square across from his building, took a paperback from her handbag and waited.

CHAPTER SEVEN

Waiting was not exactly Jackie's favorite way of passing time, and not even the good Sandra Brown novel could keep her entertained. Her eyes moved from the book to the front of the building every few seconds, and finally, at five o'clock she decided to make her move.

Crossing the street casually, she entered the building and looked for the doorman. To her surprise he was not around, so she took the elevator to the eighth floor and once there, she opened the stairs exit and went down three floors to Lieberman's. She opened the door carefully and looked at the empty marble hall. No one. Jackie gave out a sigh and walked towards the attorney's door. Just in case, she knocked on it – one never knows what could have happened during the time she came into the building and to his door, but there was no answer. Taking her tool kit from her handbag, Jackie had the door open in sixty seconds flat. Piece of shit! She said to herself going into the apartment. He should be more careful; anyone could try to break in. Then she smiled at her thoughts.

Her espadrilles didn't make any sound in the apartment, and she went through every room fast. The bathroom was next to the bedroom, and she thought he'd be taking his shower in it. His office had a large window to the side of the building, and his bedroom had one with another balcony that faced the back of it.

She chose to hide in the inside corner of the L-shaped column in the living room because she figured that unless he was looking for something in that particular place, he would not even go close to it, especially because she knew he'd be in a hurry to go kiss the Governor's ass.

It was five-twenty. The revolver in her hand, Jackie's spine was straight against the wall and her breathing was steady. Come on, Otis, hurry home! Five-thirty and she was ready to start singing 'ninety-nine bottles of beer on the wall...' when she heard the key opening the front door. She heard him come in and leave his briefcase on the floor by the kitchen door, went into the kitchen and opened the fridge, put some ice cubes into a glass and then the noise of a drink pouring into the glass.

He was whistling softly and walked towards his bedroom, the drink still in his hand because she could hear the ice clicking inside. Damn the man! More of that noise would make her for sure want to go pee.

There was silence when he got to his bedroom, and suddenly Jackie heard the noise of the shower being turned on. Another moment and she heard him going into the shower and closing the glass door. At that time she moved towards the bathroom.

Otis Lieberman was really looking forward to the party at the Governor's. He wished he had had the time to call and ask the secretary who else would be there, but, hell! he didn't mind being surprised. And surprised he was when suddenly the glass shower door opened and a woman appeared there with a small gun in her hands. He tried to close the water but she was faster, and shot him in the middle of the forehead. He fell in the shower and his blood mixed with the hot water and went down the drain, like a bad reproduction of that famous Hitchcock movie.

Jackie looked down at the body, shut off the water, closed the glass door and made her way towards the bedroom. She took her skirt off, turned around to a flowery blue print, changed the T-shirt to a blue vest, the brown wig to a blonde one, and with a last look to Lieberman's floor to see if she had accidentally dropped something, walked towards the front door. Everything took less than four minutes. She took the stairs to the eight floor and from there the elevator to the lobby, where she saw the doorman talking to two older ladies. He didn't even look at her because the ladies were asking him what happened to a package that FedEx had brought that afternoon for them.

"You go and look in that back room of yours, Tony, and I'll make you responsible if it isn't there!"

The harassed doorman asked them to wait for a second, and at that moment Jackie left the building. She walked the three blocks to the hotel without hurrying, retrieved her car from the parking basement, and once in the street, drove straight to the airport where her father's plane was waiting.

It wasn't even seven-thirty when she boarded the plane and told Rick Milano that she was ready to leave.

CHAPTER EIGHT

The Chicago heat was as bad as New Orleans and Boston. Jackie's first thought was to get back in the plane and ask Rick to fly her somewhere in the Southern Hemisphere and just leave her there until December. Unfortunately she couldn't do that, so, putting her handbag over her shoulder, she walked fast through the hot tarmac towards the private terminal that those with private jets used. She let Rick carry her bag and when they both saw Dino standing by the door, Rick gave the younger man Jackie's bag, said good-bye to her, and took another door on his left. "I hope the air conditioning is working, Dino," smiled Jackie at the chauffeur."

"Always, Signorina… Here, let me carry your handbag." Dino had been in love with Jackie since he came from Italy four years ago, and Jackie knew about it, but, as she didn't believe in teasing anyone, had never taken advantage of that love. He took her handbag and opened the limo's door for her, putting the bag on the seat by her. "There is lemonade in the bar, Signorina."

Her eyes were already closed and he shut the car door softly, taking his place on the driver's seat. The limo pulled noiselessly from the curb and soon joined the horde going to downtown Chicago and other suburbs. Dino looked at Jackie a few times during the trip but didn't dare to say anything thinking that she must be tired. All of a sudden she opened her eyes and said, "Did you say there's lemonade here, Dino?"

"Yes, Signorina. I prepared a full bottle just for you," and winked at her through the mirror. She smiled and leaned over to open the bar. A large jar of lemonade with ice was there, and she filled two of the glasses with the cool drink, giving one to Dino.

"Oh, Signorina, I shouldn't drink while I drive! Signor Quaglia will have my skin if I cause an accident."

"Don't worry about my father, Dino. And...if he ever does anything to you he'll have to deal with me. Here, take the drink." And because they were standing in traffic anyway, Dino took the glass that she was offering. They were in the same spot for more than two minutes, and finally the traffic broke and they could continue.

"We are going to my apartment, right Dino?"

"Yes, Signorina. Mr. Quaglia is not in town..."

"Really? Where is he?" Tony hadn't said anything about not being in Chicago when she got back.

"I don't know, Signorina. He left yesterday morning in the jet and told me to be waiting for him tomorrow morning around ten." He shrugged a very Italian shrug but kept his eyes on the road.

Strange, she thought. Tony usually tells me when he's leaving town... But she didn't worry. She leaned back on the plush seat and closed her eyes again. She could sleep for three days without interruption, but knew better than that. Business always came first for her father, and she was sure that, no matter where he was at this moment, he'd call her as soon as she got back to her apartment. She pressed the icy glass against her forehead. The cool felt wonderful against her skin and the drink felt better when it hit her stomach. Jackie could feel Dino's eyes on her and wondered if the young man knew what she did during those short travels out of town, not that it mattered, but sometimes she wondered how much did her father's staff knew about her and her role within 'the family'. She closed her eyes again and Dino kept his eyes on the road ahead of them.

They were soon on Lake Shore Drive and her apartment building. Dino stopped the car in the underground garage and she gave him the key to the elevator door, which would take her straight to her floor. Being the owner of the building had its advantages, and the sole use of the underground elevator was one of them. The rest of the tenants had to climb a short flight of steps to use the elevator in the lobby that would take them to their own floors.

She spent the rest of the time until late evening cleaning up her gun, taking a long bath, and phoning her father's house to speak with his assistant, but couldn't find out where Tony was. Too late to call Ireland, she went to bed almost at midnight and think about her plans to leave her duties – and how to go about it.

The next morning she woke up with the ringing of the telephone, and realized that it was the line to Aidan.

"Hallo?" his voice was like a purr in her ears. "Is that you Jackie?"

"Of course, who else?" She put a smile in her voice.

"How are you, love?" She loved it when he called her 'love'…

"I'm well, Aidan, and you?" She had his photograph in front of her, one he had sent her when they decided to exchange photos and real names, his handsome face and grin winning her over once more.

"Busy… but well. We had a close case this morning and I was gone from six until about two hours ago, but heard your message."

"Really? Would you feel like talking about it?"

"Oh, just a very hard delivery. One of the farmers' cows, we almost lost her, but fortunately all went well after a while."

"I figured you were out when I rang your office and your house and couldn't find you."

"Sorry, love... I would have loved chatting with you."

"It's all right. We are chatting now. And... that brings me to something else; how would you like me to visit you in a couple of days?"

"Really? Do you mean it?" Jackie could hear the gladness in his voice.

"Yes, I do mean it this time. My father is not going to talk me out of it..."

"That would be lovely! In fact, I was planning on taking a few days off because right before this problem this morning, my workload hadn't been too heavy, and I know that if I don't take the time now it would be too late when the sheep start to have their babies..."

Jackie laughed at his choice of words. "It's all right, you may use your vet lingo if you want. I'm sure I'll understand."

"What? A city dweller like you?" His voice sounded relaxed.

"I'm not that bad. So, what do you think? Shall I make my plans?"

"Absolutely! Just tell me when and I'll be at the airport waiting for you."

"All right. I'll make my reservations and will call you back with the flight times. It will be about three hours or so, OK with you?"

"Lovely! In the meantime I'll make arrangements for Bryan to take over for me. How long are you planning to stay? A week, two, the rest of your life…?"

She smiled a wider smile and lowered her voice. "You lovely person… let's say a week for now. I'm buying an open return ticket just in case."

"Really?"

"Really… unless you object."

"Not in your life! You may stay for as long as you wish. All the critters out there will have to live without me."

"I can never be that mean to one of your critters, as you call them."

They spoke for a few more minutes and then Jackie said she'd better get busy making the arrangements, and he was more than happy with it.

When they had started to chat through the Internet and they told each other their real names, Jackie had chosen to use the alias she planned to use once she broke away from Tony. All her papers under that name were good and real, and she had kept her name of Jackie because it would be easy for her.

She called a travel agent she knew and the woman arranged a flight for her to Shannon two days from today. Tony would have to live with that decision, she thought, and no matter what he'd say, she was going to Ireland. An hour later all her arrangements had been made. She had a first class ticket waiting at O'Hare and she'd be leaving at around 7:30 PM, getting into Shannon at 10:30 AM the next day. It would be nice to use Tony's jet this time, but she knew it was impossible. She'd have to learn not to be spoilt by her father's riches and travel like the rest of mankind. Or womankind.

She danced towards her bedroom and opened the closet where her personal safe was and opening it, she took a large envelope containing a passport, driver's license, and three major credit cards in the name of Jacqueline Millard – the name given to Aidan. All her identification papers were good and up to date, and nobody knew she had them – not even Tony. Especially Tony!, she thought, he'd kill her with his own hands if he knew. But he was not going to know. She made sure of that. If she could go all over the world doing his work and had not been found out, she could easily go to Ireland and disappear for a couple of weeks without having to report to him or anyone else. The only problem she saw right now was to tell him that she was going to be unavailable for that time, but she hadn't been president of the debate class in high school for nothing!

The call from Tony came at noon that day. "Hey, kid! How are ya? Was everything OK down south?"

"Hi, Tony! Yes, everything went according to plan. What about the second part of the plan?" She meant the rescue of Vito Vanieri and Mark Pollietto, the two members of the 'family' that were being held in Louisiana.

"That's why I'm out of town right now, Jackie. Your work was finished right on time, I'm happy to say, because Vito's and Mark's date in court was moved ahead a couple of days and we caught them just in time. They're both on their way to a safe house as we speak."

"How did you find out about the change of days in court?"

A low laugh was heard on the other side of the line. "Money talks loud and clear, Jackie. The person who has been keeping us informed of their situation gave us a call as soon as he heard, and we had to move fast."

"Silly me. So, when are you getting back?"

"In an hour's time. You gonna be home tonight?"

"I was planning to…"

"Why don't you come to dinner at the house? We have to talk."

Oh-oh. "Tony… You promised there would be no more work for me for at least one month."

"Don't jump at my throat! Who said I was going to give you more work?"

"You didn't, but I know you, Tony." She paused but he didn't say anything, so she continued, "and remember you promised me a bonus for this last job."

"I remember, I remember! That's one of the reasons why I want you at the house tonight."

"That's one of the reasons. What's the other one?"

"You wait until tonight, OK? You'll like it."

"Yeah, right! Can hardly wait."

"Jackie..." his voice was low, "has anyone told you that you are getting very sassy?"

"As far as I know, I've always been sassy, Tony. It's the only way to deal with bastards like you."

"Watch your mouth, girlie, this is your father here."

"There's only one thing I have to say to you, Tony: no more jobs for at least a month. I have plans and I am going to go ahead with them. And... father dear, they don't include you or my work. Is that clear?"

Tony had been around long enough to know that in this world full of buttons, there are some one should not push, so he just mumbled something incoherent, gave her a fast 'see ya later' and disconnected the call. Jackie looked at the mute receiver in her hand, and put it down with a smile. She was on her way to Ireland to meet a wonderful person and nobody – neither her father nor the Lord himself were going to stop her.

CHAPTER NINE

Life is certainly not easy when one is the daughter of Tony Quaglia, and Jackie's had been tinted with the knowledge that her father was a dangerous man in the best of times, and that crossing him and getting away with it was not easy task for anybody. She didn't want to go against his will, but at the same time, the time she had set for herself to get away from that dreaded life was getting shorter since she met Aidan Cassidy.

It was near three in the afternoon when her doorbell rang and she knew even before she opened it, that it was Tony. She saw herself reflected in the hallway mirror on her way to the front door and winked at herself, putting at the same time, a smile on her face.

When she opened the door, Tony was standing there. "Are you sure this door is strong enough?"

"I'm just fine, Father... what about you?"

Tony looked at her and softened his expression. "Like I said, Jackie, you are getting more sassy as days go by." He leaned over her and kissed her cheek. "You OK kid?"

"Yes, of course I'm OK. Thanks for asking. May I ask you at what do I owe the pleasure of your personal visit to my humble abode? And strong enough for what? – I mean, my door…"

Tony had to laugh at her lengthy speech. "Jackie, cut the crap. You know very well that I worry about you living alone here in this mausoleum. Why don't you move to the big house with me?"

"God forbids, Tony! Why in the world should I do such thing? And this mausoleum, as you graciously call it, overlooks Lake Michigan."

"Lake Michigan is not the Sea of Galilee… Anyway, tell me about New Orleans. Was it hard?"

"Better than I thought it would be. Attorneys are so predictable I knew his daily movements once I followed him for a couple of hours. It was easier than quite a few other hits I can remember."

"Good. Mark and Vito are safely out of the country. I took them to Toronto"…he pronounced it Trawno, "and from there they're going to Italy, then I hope they'll stay put in Milan for a couple of years." He sat in one of her comfortable chairs in the living room and took a cigar from his pocket.

"Not in my house, Tony. I've told you a million times I hate the smell of your cigars."

"But these are from Cuba!"

"I don't care if Fidel himself sent them to you from Fuckcity! No smoking in my house!" She took the cigar from her father's hands and put it on the table behind her. Tony looked at it, then moved around in his chair. "OK, tell me what this noise is all about."

"What noise?" She looked at him, fearing he was going to say something about Aidan. But how could he guess?

"About your vacation. You told me not to give you any more jobs for a month... What are your plans?"

"And I meant it. I'm going to Argentina for four weeks."

"Argentina! What the fuck did you loose in Argentina? It's full of Nazis!"

"Tony... There were Nazis back in the 50s and 60s. They were all caught and sent to Nuremberg to be tried. Didn't you see the movie? I want to go there because it's nice, it's winter now and the heat here is killing me."

"Well, can't you go somewhere here in the good ole US of A?"

"No, Tony, I don't want to stay here." She paused for a moment, then lowered her voice, "Tony, I need a vacation. Trust me. I'll be gone maybe three weeks, but not more than a month, I promise you..."

He was quiet for a moment, then said, "OK, just leave the name of the hotel just in case I need to speak with you."

Jackie hesitated for just a moment. "It's the Grand Hotel in Buenos Aires." She had no idea if there was a Grand Hotel in Buenos Aires, but every large city has one anyway, so she figured she couldn't go wrong. If she could make noises as if she was really going to Argentina, that'd be the first place he'd look for her if he needed her, but she was sure he'd never think of Ireland. Then all of a sudden she had a thought. "Tony, you don't have another job for me, do you?" And before he answered she knew what the reply would be. "Oh, hell of hells, Tony! Not another one! You promised me when I got back from Boston that the New Orleans job would be it and then I could go. I have all my arrangements made and am not going to postpone them, is that clear? Go ask someone else..." but her curiosity got the best of her. "Where is it this time?"

"Dallas. An easy job, but if you cannot do it it's just fine. I'll get one of the boys to go." He knew that a few months ago the old Jackie would have put aside her vacation, but wasn't too sure about today's Jackie – and he was right.

"Well, it's about time someone else helps you, Tony. Right now my stress level is so tight I can explode at any minute, and my thinking processes are so sluggish as to be almost immobile."

"No one is as good as you are, Jackie."

"I know that", she said without humility, "and just because I'm good you have to realize that you don't have the right to over-work me. Now, did you put the money for these last two jobs in my account?"

"Of course! Vince did it a couple of days ago. Sixty-thousand grand."

She made a quick calculation in her mind and nodded. "That sounds right, and just as we had agreed. So tell me, have you seen the news about Lieberman's death already?"

"In the Internet this morning. Apparently his girlfriend came by and found him in the shower... Why the shower, anyway?"

Jackie shrugged. "It was the safest place at the time. Not near the telephones or to anything that could have been used as a weapon, unless you count a bar of soap and a yellow rubber ducky..."

Tony laughed. "You're shitting me! A rubber duck?"

"The truth! I bet the papers didn't mention it...."

Tony was still laughing. "They sure didn't! Well, like I told you, it was done just in time because Vito and Mark were going back to court before the date they had before."

"How did the abduction go?"

"Pretty good, just as planned too. There were other prisoners in the van, but we didn't touch them. The driver got a shiner and an egg on top of his head, but no blood was spilled. No use killing the bastard once we got him asleep."

"No patrol cars following the van?"

"Nothin'. I told you they had them in a cow town close to Orleans."

He looked at his watch. "Well, kid, better get going." He came closer to her and hugged her. "Have a safe trip and come back as soon as you get bored."

Fat chance., she thought, and aloud she said, "Thanks, Tony. I'll send you a postcard. And I take it then that you won't need to see me tonight in the big house?"

"No. Just to show you how much I love you...Rossi is going to be there and I know how much the two of you love each other... So-long Jackie. Take care." He left the apartment in a flurry of words in Italian, still unhappy with her vacation plans but too clever to show too much.

Jackie dropped in the chair he had been using, and sighed. "Thank you, God! It was easier than I thought." Next, she sat at the kitchen table and made a list of all the things she had to take care of before leaving – among them, a shopping trip to Marshall Fields to stock up on summer dresses, and another to Victoria's Secret for teddies and other lacy things. She grinned and thought about calling Aidan, but controlled herself and got a cold drink from the fridge instead.

When that was done she sat in front of her computer and got into the Internet, where she called a New Orleans page to read about attorney Otis Lieberman's untimely death. *"There are no clues"*, she read, *"about the person or persons who entered Assistant District Attorney Otis Liberman's apartment in Lafayette Square and shot him while he was taking a shower. The doorman of the building, Anthony Porter, didn't see anyone entering or leaving the lobby prior to the attorney's girlfriend Sheila Banks who found the man's body at 6:35 PM when she came to pick him up to go to a reception at the Governor's mansion. The strange thing was that the Governor's personnel denied that a reception of any kind was being held at the mansion that evening, but Lieberman's secretary assured this reporter that the invitation had come the day before through the telephone. When asked if a man or a woman had called, the secretary – who has been with Lieberman for four years – said that she couldn't recall as it had been an extremely busy day, but she had written the name 'Megan' at the end of the message, therefore there's good reason to believe that the caller had been a woman pretending she was in the Governor's employ."*

The reporter ended the article listing Lieberman's career and the fact that he was one of the most promising attorneys at the D.A's office.

Jackie didn't make a copy of the article or thought about it any longer. She typed "Ireland" in her browser and chose one of the many web sites under that heading, reading as much as she could about Aidan's country. She was going to make herself knowledgeable about as much as she could, and show him that Americans are not – as the world believes – the product of a careless and superficial form of education.

She made copies of several pages and sat in her comfortable living room, sipping a cold drink and already assimilating the Celtic way of life, the latest developments in her life completely forgotten, the way she had been trained.

CHAPTER TEN

The plane lifted off from O'Hare International Airport after taxiing faster and faster through the hot runway, and Jackie was pushed back against the soft leather of her first class seat by the pressure in the cabin. The sun was still shining over the Midwest even though it was already past seven-thirty in the afternoon of yet another hot day. She closed her eyes and made a mental note of the many items she had to take care of before leaving Chicago, and mentally crossed them as she went by each one of them. Jackie wanted her time in Ireland to be free from the anxiety that usually filled her days in Chicago. God knows she needed this holiday!, and meeting Aidan was the icing to the cake.

Aidan. If things **went** well between them and he asked her to stay she was going to accept – to hell with the consequences her action would bring upon her head. As she had traveled with a passport unknown to Tony, the chances of him finding her were close to nonexistent, and she could always travel back to see him and try to explain. 'Try to explain' was the right use of words, because deep in her heart she knew that Tony would never understand her feelings for someone like Aidan – a common man who actually worked for a living, and someone who saved lives – albeit animal lives – to boot. There was also the problem of telling Aidan about her real life. Would she dare to tell him? No, of course she wouldn't! He was noble, good, generous, and all together wonderful. She and her family were killers of men, some of them – she knew – as noble and good as Aidan himself.

She moved in her seat, as if she were seated on a pillow of pins and needles, and the flight attendant came almost running to ask her if she needed anything. Jackie told her she was all right and moved her face towards the window, moving the gray plastic shade up to see a blue sky and fluffy clouds way below.

She stayed in that position until the plane leveled off and the flight attendant came by and brought her a drink and a small tray with small sandwiches, dainty and delicious. Jackie looked at them for a long time and finally took one, together with a sip of very good white wine. She was jumping ahead of herself thinking that Aidan would ask her to stay in Ireland. What if he didn't really like her in person? Although she already knew he did because he had told her so many times, there was always the possibility that they didn't get along well at all...

Choices... One's entire life was a question of choices, and Jackie Quaglia had made all the wrong ones from the beginning. If she had had the courage to leave Tony years ago she would not be in this predicament right now, but first it was the matter of her mother being alive, then, after her premature death it was Tony and the hold that he put on her. But she had done her time as far as following her father's wishes was concerned, and now it was her time to live the life she wanted. Even if this budding relationship with Aidan didn't work out, she'd still get away from Tony for good. Jackie was very sure of it and nothing would change her mind. He crossed her fingers as that thought came to mind.

CHAPTER ELEVEN

It was a long flight but Jackie couldn't sleep. When the pilot announced that they would be landing in Dublin on their way to Shannon, she waited until all the passengers deplaned and went into the lavatory to freshen up by washing her face and applying new make-up. She put her long hair in a loose bun on top of her head and thought she looked pretty good for someone who had been fighting stomach butterflies for seven hours. When she got back to her seat, she noticed that some on the passengers that would be going on to Shannon were back in the plane, and about fifteen minutes later they were on their way once more. The short flight to the western Irish capital was enough for her to wish she were back in Chicago. What if Aidan didn't like her after all? The thought came coming back to her mind. Naw... Jackie knew herself enough to realize that any man would be proud to have her by his side. What if he hadn't been able to take days off and she were left alone to sightsee? Bad, but she could certainly go on her own. What if he had been lying to her and he was actually a 70-gnarled years old with no teeth and bad breath? Now that would be pretty bad. What if he was married? That, on the other hand, would be horrible. She smiled at her thought and the flight attendant came to where she was.

"I noticed you didn't get any sleep last night, are you all right?"

Jackie felt like talking to another woman. "In a way... I'm meeting someone for the first time and my stomach is a mess. I was making scenarios in my mind where he is anything but what I think he is."

The other woman sat with her. "Well, we have flights back every day," she smiled a wider smile. "So you haven't met him in person?"

"Right. We met through a group of people and we have been writing for quite some time, but I'm afraid... One reads so many cases when these things happen..."

"Did you meet through the Internet?" Now, how in the world...?

Jackie felt a pang, but her face didn't show it. She was not going to tell anyone the way she had met Aidan. "Oh, no! He's a friend of friends, but we have been e-mailing and telephoning. He did send me his photo, though, and he's really gorgeous... but I was just thinking what if he sent me someone else's photo, or he's married, or 117 years old...?"

The flight attendant laughed out loud and some people turned their heads to where they were sitting. "Oh, you are too much! But just in case, remember we have a return flight tomorrow at 1:00 PM and you'll be tucked in your own bed by evening, Chicago time." She patted Jackie's hand and got up. "Don't fret right now. He'll be everything you envisioned, and probably more…" she winked and Jackie's fears went away. "I'll guess you're right. I can afford twelve hours to give him. He sounds so wonderful that I doubt he's anything but marvelous. Just having kittens, that's all."

"You'll be fine. I hope I'm on your return flight and you can tell me all."

"Deal," said Jackie and shook the other woman's hand with both of hers.

Shannon airport was not as large as others that Jackie had visited, but busy enough to get lost if one doesn't know where to go. Before deplaning, she checked her beige linen suit and saw that although the skirt was a bit wrinkled, the rest of it was nice looking. Her face was nicely made up and her hair in place. Only her hands were shaking. Get over this, Jackie! she said to herself. You haven't been this nervous since…when? She couldn't even recall the last time when butterflies had nested in her stomach for this long.

Jackie took her handbag and started to walk towards the passport-checking booth. A pale young man asked for her passport, reason to visit Ireland, and length of stay and she answered without hesitation. Apparently everything was all right because he gave her a wan smile and said in a monotonous voice, "Welcome to the Republic of Ireland, Miss. Have a pleasant stay."

She gave him her killer smile – the real one – and walked away. Getting her luggage was easy and fast and then she saw herself walking on rubber legs towards the exit. There were lots of people waiting for arriving passengers, some with signs stating a name, others with flowers, and she stood still looking around and trying to figure out where, among those strangers, was Aidan, and soon found out when a tall man in a gray suit appeared from her right. He was carrying a large bouquet of white roses in his left hand, his right was waving at her from the back of the waiting line. God, he was gorgeous! She recognized his face from the photos they had exchanged and smiled broadly at him. When he came closer and stood by her she noticed that his eyes were the bluest they had ever seen, his hair not as dark as she thought but rather a dark brown, and that he had a small dimple on the left side of his mouth.

"Hello, darling!" he said and took her into his arms in a warm embrace. He then kissed her on both cheeks, very continental, and after that put her in front of him. "Did the cat eat your tongue?"

"No, he didn't. I'm so glad I'm here, Aidan! So glad to finally meet you in person!"

He didn't answer. Instead, he leaned over and kissed her lips softly.

"Aye, it has been quite some time since I was so eager to meet someone, Jackie girl. Come on, I can see that you have your luggage, and let's get out of this place. Welcome to Ireland!"

"Thanks! It's nice to get out of the Chicago heat."

Their conversation became general as they fetched her luggage and later walked towards the entrance. His car, a Volvo 4-door, was parked near the entrance and there was already a constable looking it over, writing pad in hand. Aidan talked to him for a moment and the man walked away shaking his head.

"What did you say to him?" asked Jackie, "Are policemen in Ireland always that nice?"

"No. I told him I was a vet and there was a very sick canine inside."

She smiled. "This must be the first proof of the famous 'luck of the Irish' I hear so much in the States. Either that or the story of the Blarney stone…"

He stopped for a moment. "You know…we Irish always ask ourselves what does that mean and nobody has been able to find an answer…so it has to be the Blarney stone."

They both laughed and got in the car. Aidan drove carefully through the airport and once on the road he started to point places of interest in his charming Irish accent. His left hand was holding Jackie's as he drove carefully on the left side of the road. Jackie had been enough times in the UK to know their way of driving and traffic laws, and didn't get nervous as someone else's might have, instead, she smiled at him and looked at the sites out of politeness. Aidan lived in the very Ring of Kerry, in a whitewashed cottage with thatched roof set about one hundred feet from the ocean, on a hill that overlooked miles and miles of gorgeous shores. Jackie held her breath. "Oh, Aidan! This is heavenly!"

He looked at her and smiled that smile of his. "A Chicagoan calling my little cottage 'heavenly'? Are you teasing me?"

"Never! I'd never tease you...well, not this way, anyway." They both laughed, and she continued, "It's the setting, the house, the Atlantic Ocean right at your feet... Have you always lived here?"

"Yes, for quite some time now. My parents' house is right around the bend, over there..." he pointed to his left, "and this piece of land used to belong to them. When I started my practice they gave it to me and I remodeled the cottage. You should have seen it before! No roof, the walls were falling down...you name it. It took me nearly a year to finish it."

Jackie was fascinated not only with him and his personality but also with his voice; his Irish inflection was beautiful and she didn't tire of listening to him. "I'll show you everything after we get to the house. You may want to freshen up, then we can have a nice cup of tea and if you are not tired I'll show you around."

"I'd love that," she said. He parked the car on the side of the house and got out, coming around and helping her. When she was out of the car, he opened the back door and took her luggage. "You travel light, I can see…"

"A change from my business trips," she said, "I only brought one dressy dress, and the rest is just everyday things. And, because I plan to shop, I figure that if I need something I can always buy it."

"Spoken like a true woman!" His hand went around her waist as he guided her towards the house. She noticed that the door was unlocked.

"Do you leave the door unlocked or there's someone here?" Oh, God! What if he said, yes, my wife…

But he didn't. Instead he laughed, "This is not Chicago. I always leave my door unlocked, and nothing has ever happened…"

She rolled her eyes. "Just like home," she said and they laughed again. "I locked my door even if I have to downstairs to speak to the doorman. I have three locks plus an alarm, and my father is always asking me if I feel secure."

"He loves you very much, I'm sure…" Oh, Aidan, if you only knew… "I have seen movies showing New York flats and I can see that they have quite a few locks too."

"Yes, unfortunately it is that way. I hear that there are still small towns where people don't lock, but they are getting rarer and rarer all the time…" She looked around the house. They were standing in a small hallway that had a staircase on the left, and a door right before it. There was another door on the right and she could see a sitting room with a fireplace and deep beige furniture. The door on the left was closed and when Aidan opened it to let her in, she saw a dining room with heavy furniture that seemed to be quite old but had the patina of years and years of elbow wax. It smelled faintly of lemon and some spice she couldn't pinpoint. At the end of the room there was an arch door leading to the kitchen, a large room that seemed to be the heart of the house. Although it had modern stainless steel appliances, the cabinets were almost a match to the dining room furniture, and she made a comment about that.

"It's a long story," he said, "the furniture used to belong to my great-grandparents – it's ancient! – and these cabinets are of the same wood but made about six years ago by the best carpenter in Ireland: my good childhood friend Patrick O'Faolian. He has taken many prices not only here and in Britain, but also in the continent. I'll take you to his shop."

"Oh, yes! I'd love to see his work!"

"I knew you'd say that!" He said and showed her a chair by the scrubbed table in the middle of the kitchen. "Sit down, please, while I get the tea things ready."

"Do you know me that well?"

He stopped in the middle of reaching the tea from one of the cabinets. "I think I do, Jackie…We have been communicating for some time now and I think we have touched every theme in the book. I know your likes and dislikes, and one of your likes is antique furniture and cabinetry work. Remember you told me about that place in Northern Illinois called Galena where you bought your desk?"

Her eyes opened wide. "You remember that? Yes, I did buy it there at the spur of the moment. I was there...looking around..." I was there following Senator Castle and his lover... "and when I saw it in the window of an antiques shop I had to go in and buy it."

"See? I have the memory of an elephant, so, if you don't want me to remind you of something naughty thirty years from now, don't tell me."

She liked his mention of 'thirty years from now' but didn't say anything. Instead she put a mock look of horror on her face. "Oh dear, what else did I tell you?"

His eyebrows went up and down like Groucho's. "Many, many things..."

"I guess I'll have to be careful with you..." You can't imagine how careful!

They had their tea and chatted about many other things. Once finished, she put everything in the dishwasher and said, "All right, let me go freshen up and then you can take me places."

He led her upstairs to a bedroom that was obviously his. It was masculine, done in blue and beige, with an enormous four poster. "Don't tell me your friend made this bed also…" she said, trying to hide her confusion at the sight of the bed.

"No, that also belonged to my great-grandparents. I changed the bottom and had the legs cut down a bit, but the rest is the original." He went to the left of the room and opened a door. "Here's the bathroom; we have plenty of hot water so please don't worry about its use. Just come downstairs when you are ready. And, Jackie…welcome to my home." This was said in almost a whisper. Before she could react he had left the room, closing the heavy door behind him.

Jackie sat on the bed and looked at the window that faced the side of the house. The enormous expand of the Atlantic Ocean was before her eyes, and the sun put diamonds on its surface which was unmovable, with only faint white waves breaking on the shore.

"It's like a dream!" she said aloud…"Please God, let it last!"

With a sigh she opened her suitcase and took out a pair of white jeans and a silk blouse the colour of the Irish sky and, walking to the well-appointed bathroom, took a quick shower. Putting fresh make-up and a fast brushing of her long hair took only a couple of minutes and she was soon walking down the stairs. She found Aidan in the sitting room with a portable telephone on his ear. She was talking to someone about a horse and she stood behind him, listening to his incredible voice tell the other person how to feed the animal the pills he had prescribed. When he finished his conversation he turned around and smiled at Jackie. "These people! If they can't find me in the surgery they call me here. I did tell my secretary to say I was very busy today, but somehow the man found me. Sorry about that, Jackie."

"Please, don't say that!" She came closer and put her hands on his. "I'm the one imposing on your life…"

"Never! Don't say that! I'm elated to have you here." He then took her face in his two hands and kissed her. It wasn't a soft, shy kiss, but one full of all the longing he had for her, something she didn't know yet.

Jackie came closer to him and put her arms around his waist, and after the kiss was over, he held her very tightly but didn't say anything. Jackie looked up at his face and saw that his eyes were closed. "You all right?" she asked quietly.

He shook his head and said, "Of course, it's just a dream come true to have you here." He kissed her again, and after a while, added, "We better go or I'll have to take you upstairs and…"

She interrupted him, "And show me that Ireland is indeed the ancient birthplace of good times?"

"Exactly! So, let's get going."

He took her everywhere in his area. She saw that even Ireland's most remote corners fill up with tour buses this time of the year and at times the travel was a bumper-to-bumper crawl, but Aidan's intelligent conversation kept her wishing the day would never end. But end it did, and soon it was dinnertime. He stopped at a quaint country inn and they found a table that a talkative couple from the South of the United States – Jackie recognized the accent – had just left vacant. They sat after it was cleared by the jolly waitress and were offered the dish of the day: grilled wild Irish salmon in a bed of new potatoes, carrots and tarragon. For dessert, they had – of all things! – tiramisu, the most tasty Italian dessert ever created. They followed everything with a cup of strong coffee that Jackie knew would keep her awake all night. Hmmm, she thought, not a bad idea! And she inwardly giggled.

The drive back to the cottage, as Aidan called his house, was a bit faster than the previous one because it was already dark, and when they arrived, Aidan told her to sit in the sitting room. He went to the long piece of furniture he had against the wall opposite the sofa, and soon came back with two glasses of Remy Martin, giving one to Jackie, who wondered if he remembered her taste or it was just a coincidence.

"Cheers," he said, touching her glass with his. "To us, and to an unforgettable stay in Ireland."

"Cheers," she said and took a sip. The drink burned her throat and she remembered other times when she had just come back home from one of her many trips and the first thing done was to fill a glass of the delicious spirit. But no! No more of those thoughts! She was with Aidan, in Ireland, in his house, and thoughts like those were not welcome.

"You've gone pensive on me...any problems?" His face was very close to hers.

"Oh, no...I was just...overwhelmed, thinking about this day. I love it here. Not only the scenery but also the way people are and behave. And you..." she touched his chin and lips, "you are everything I thought you would be, and more."

"Really? Aren't you afraid that I'm really a psychopath who has lured you here to have you at my mercy and have my wicked way with you?"

"I hope so..." she answered and they both laughed. "Aidan, you don't have a wicked bone in your body."

He looked at the ceiling. "Right. That is true, I think...but I do want to have my wicked way with you."

"No time like the present...", was her reply and got up, pulling him by the hand.

CHAPTER TWELVE

How Jackie lived through that first evening in Ireland was beyond words. Aidan was the perfect lover, the one who gives pleasure before taking his own and she felt cherished from the moment their bodies touched his soft bed in the second floor of the cottage, right underneath the eaves. They made love the rest of the night and it was dawn when she felt his peaceful breathing caress the top of her head. She was laying almost on top of him, with her head resting on his chest and her right arm around his waist. The last he said to him was, "I didn't have a life until today, Jackie…" then there was silence and she realized he had fallen asleep. He was one of those peaceful sleepers, with no noises coming from nose or mouth; he looked as if he was just resting there with his eyes closed.

As always, that was the time of night when her demons started to gnaw her heart and her entire life passed before her eyes, just like the way people say happens when one is in deep danger. She felt hot tears slide down her smooth cheeks and the fear of waking him up prevented her from wipe them clean. She didn't know how long she was there, eyes wide open and soul completely given to a handsome vet in Ireland's Ring of Kerry coast. She realized it wasn't a question of incredible sex but rather the fact that he had shown her so much care and love! He had given himself to her through the cold screen of her computer a few months before. His stories about himself and his family, his struggle to keep himself in medical school in spite of his father's wish for him to follow on his steps, his first love, "a colleen that left me because I didn't have a posh car" said in that beautiful Irish lilt of his (the woman had been an asshole, but Jackie was grateful to her anyway), and his wish to take care of Jackie and to provide for her every wish. God, she thought, I could buy this entire village if I wanted! But of course, she couldn't say those words aloud. She started to feel a kink on her shoulder and moved a bit to the side and the movement woke him up. His incredible blue eyes became soft when he saw her on his chest, and he placed a small kiss on her head. "Good morning..." he said.

"Good morning, Aidan...did you sleep well?"

"How can I not sleep well? If I had died in my sleep it would take twenty morticians to erase the smile from my lips."

They both laughed. "How can anyone tell jokes so early in the morning?," she asked him, moving up over his body until their faces were together.

"Beats me! I didn't use to be this way yesterday. Must be my bedfellow." His hands were caressing her back from neck to buttocks and she moved slowly a few times. "You tickle me," she teased knowing exactly what she was doing to him.

"Too bad."

"Well, I'll have to get mean and give you exactly three hours to stop it."

"And if I don't?"

"Then I'll have to add a few more hours to make you understand that I mean business."

"And you really scare me, you know?"

"You should be scared!" Oh, Aidan…

"Why don't we just make lots of love right now and maybe then I'll learn my lesson?"

"Why don't we?"

It was ten in the morning when they decided to get up.

"Did you learn your lesson?," she asked him while they showered together.

"What lesson? I guess I forgot to tell you that I'm the village idiot." he teased her, rubbing her breasts.

Jackie threw her head back and laughed for a long time. It was so easy to talk with him, his mind was so fast and his wit was equaled to that of his countryman Oscar Wilde – who happened to be her old time favorite author.

After their shower he cooked breakfast and Jackie was surprised to see that he was a very good cook. She praised his culinary skills and helped with the washing up, and when they left the cottage again to more sightseeing, she was sitting very close to him in the car.

He took her to see the ruins of a Druid castle and the sleepy village that he called home, he showed her his "surgery" or the place where he had his office and consulting rooms, and then they stopped at the village pub to have a light lunch.

People greeted him and he waved at everybody. Some of them approached him to take a good look at Jackie who looked beautiful in a dark green summer dress and sandals. She shook hands with what looked like a million people, and smiled at them when she saw them elbowing Aidan's ribs with knowing smiles. One of them, an old man with a blue winter cap, smiled at her and said, "So ye be from Chicago, eh? I remember when I was just a wee lad when the Valentine Day's massacre happened. Nasty thing that was! But you are too young to know about those times, with Al Capone and such…"

"I was, but I know all about Al Capone," she said without adding that the small band of people that called themselves "descendants of the old Capone gang" had a price on Tony's head. They wouldn't understand, she mused.

"You do? Well, that's fresh. Nowadays kids only talk about them drugs and satanic music!"

"Anyone born and raised in Chicago knows that Capone is actually part of our city history. I have seen his tomb, next to his mother's."

"A big mausoleum, I bet…" said the old timer, listening attentively.

"No. As a matter of fact, is a small headstone with his name and dates of birth and death. His mother's is just a bit more ornate."

The man had forgotten about the glass of ale in front of him and was listening with his mouth open.

"Damn mesself to hell!" he swore and then said to Aidan. "You keep this colleen, doc. She's not only as pretty as the morning mist over the sea but clever to boot. She probably has Irish blood in her."

"I'm working on it, Paddy, and yes, I'm sure she has it…" He looked into her eyes and brought her closer to him.

They said so long to his friends and walked towards the car.

"You are loved here," she said to him.

"They like me, yes, but I bet I have been their pets vet and the only one who has pressed them to keep up with their shots."

"And you love your job," her words were slow.

"Yes, I do. Saving human lives is exceptional, but saving critters is very rewarding as well. Did you have pets when you were growing up?"

She remembered Bambolletta, the small cat that had been her companion since she was five or six. "Yes," she said smiling. "A little gray kitten that was called Bambolletta..."

"That sounds Italian," he said and she flinched. Oops!

"Yes, it's Italian. A friend of mine gave it to me and she came with that name." Vin and his wife had given her the kitten when her mother first got sick, a sickness that lingered for over ten years and finally killed her.

Their conversation turned to his work and the way he cared about his patients, about his dreams to start a large veterinary clinic with boarding facilities for different pets, including horses.

"Unfortunately that takes money," he said with a sigh. "I have tried to talk my father into donating the land that borders my cottage, but the old man is adamant. He doesn't like me being a vet and thinks that by doing that he'll kill my passion. Sometimes I'm surprised he gave me this cottage and the little land surrounding it."

"And is that a lot of money that you need?" she said nonchalantly, then remembered that the British were extremely closed about their personal information. Of course, Irish from the Republic of Ireland weren't exactly British...but pretty close.

"It is to me at this moment...I'd say close to 250 thousand pounds. Actually, I have most of it, but the running of my surgery doesn't allow me to touch that amount."

"Can't your father give you your share of your inheritance?"

"I tried that as well," he gave a sad laugh, "and I'm very close to getting it, but his conditions are hard to accept. Right now it's up to me but I'm a hard-headed bloke."

"Sometimes that's a hindrance in one's life, but most of the time it's a blessing. The opposite would be a wimp, and you ain't nothing like that!"

"Is that the way Chicagoans speak?"

"No, that's how they think." She laughed and he hugged her against him.

"But really...the old man is not bad, just stubborn. In fact, you'll meet them tonight for dinner and you can see for yourself."

"I'm meeting your parents?" He nodded.

"Of course...I just thought...well, never mind what I thought. They'd be delighted." Deep inside, Jackie sent a small prayer to St. Patrick or whoever was the saint who'd shield her against inquisitive eyes and wondering minds.

The dinner had been all right and she realized that her fears had been unfounded. Aidan's parents were a nice older couple who were rather tied to their ancestry and old customs, but interesting to talk to and very fond of their son. She answered their questions with ease and showed interest in the grand old house and its history. She had learn at an early age that if one has to get on the good side of someone, the best thing is to praise their family, house, or other possessions.

After dinner, they walked along the shore towards Aidan's cottage. The ocean was cold as it usually is that far north, but there were no waves, just a soft movement of water caressing the shore. Aidan had put his arms around her shoulders only by her – a story about the fairies and leprechauns that, according to folk tales, lived in that area, heard his voice.

She had a smile on her lips, and more than once he looked down at her face and stopped to kiss her.

"Where have you been all my life, Jackie?", he asked one of the times that they stopped to kiss.

Oh dear, you don't want to hear my answer... "Well...let's see...in a boring school for girls, then at university cramming information into my small brain, then working for my father..."

"I believe everything except the 'small brain' part. You're nothing but clever!"

She laughed and looked at the sky now filling with stars, "Thank you, God! He thinks I'm clever," she whispered to an invisible god. They laughed and he grabbed her by her waist and whirled her around. Her sandals fell in the sand and her bare feet were making round marks in the sand.

When he put her down he bent and kissed her, slowly first and then fast, greedily, with a passion that sent her mind spinning around the way her body had spun just a few minutes earlier.

When the kiss was over her arms remained around his neck, their noses touching. "Jackie..." she heard him saying, "you have bewitched me. You are just like the Faeries in this land – not only gorgeous to look at but also with a soul of many facets: playful, witty, inquisitive...I don't get tired of being with you, listening to your voice telling me stories and customs of your country..." all this was said in a whisper, and his soft Irish dialect was even more accentuated.

"The feeling is certainly mutual, Aidan. I'm going to miss you very much when I go back home. Thank God for the Internet! We have to get one of those cameras to put on top of our terminals so we can chat and see each other at the same time."

"Consider it done! But...you don't have to leave, did you know that?"

She smiled and shook her head. "Don't I know it! Unfortunately my time is not quite mine yet. My work is demanding and I belong to my father. I am, however, trying to quit."

"Really? And what will you do when you quit? Will that make him unhappy?"

"I wish it'd make him 'just' unhappy! That would be so easy! He'll give me hell...but I have plans for myself, Aidan, and quitting is priority one for me."

He looked at her for a moment. "Is there anything I can do to help? I could talk to him and tell him that I have a job for you here..."

"You do?"

"Yes, making me happy for the rest of my life. Will you stay?" His deep blue eyes were looking straight into her soul, and Jackie's knees became jelly.

She gave a small laugh. "It almost sound like a proposal for...well, for something."

"It is. I'm asking you to stay here and be my wife."

"Aidan!"

"What's the problem?"

"There is no problem... but the foundation of marriage should be love. We just met."

"We just met in person, but we have been communicating for months now. I know all about you, and you know all about me, and if you don't, all you have to do is ask. I love you."

"Aidan..." she looked into the sky and studied the great expanse of dark blue above them, then, looking at him said, "Aidan...I don't know if what I feel for you is love, but if it isn't it must the closest thing...but marriage is something that I have not foreseen for me. I have a commitment with my father, with my family, and breaking it means trouble..."

"Trouble? What do you mean?" He put her apart a few inches and a frown marked his smooth forehead. No, she couldn't possibly tell him what her words meant, so she shrugged and said, "Well, maybe not exactly trouble, but I still have things to do for my father. But...as I said before, I have plans and it will take me another couple of months to finish what I have in mind. Then, after I end my commitment I'll be able to travel back here."

"You speak as if you have some kind of a contract to fulfill..."

"No, of course not, but I gave him my word. Besides, I have an apartment in Chicago to get rid of...in fact, it's more than an apartment, it's an entire building, and before I make a move I have to make sure that's disposed of."

He kept looking at her. "Are you telling me that you are very rich and you own a building?"

She had actually three buildings in the Chicago area. "Is that a problem?"

"No, not at all...I just thought that you owned your own flat, in which case you could leave it in the hands of an estate agent and monitor its sale from here..."

How to explain to this man that her life was not hers at the moment? That she wasn't quite free to make the move? There were no words to explain her way of life. Nobody in his right mind would ever understand it, the chains that linked her to Tony and the family, the way she had to obey his demands... Her face didn't show her concerns, instead, she smiled at him and said, "I need at least two more months to finish my business in Chicago and I promise you that I'll come back. I can't leave things to be done later on. For my own peace of mind... and, because I think I have a buyer for my building all I have to do when I get back is to contact this man and see if he can do it immediately."

"And if he can't?" His voice was careful. "The last time I spoke with him he wanted to make an offer. He is one of the tenants, lives in the apartment right below mine."

"Jackie...will your father be opposed to your move?"

Is the Pope Catholic? "Yes, very much so. He wants to leave his business to me and I don't want it. We have had fighting matches because of this, and he won't take no for an answer. In fact...I have been thinking about just leaving without saying anything…"

He shook his head in disbelief. "Leaving without a word? Isn't that a bit drastic?"

"It sounds drastic, but knowing my father, he'll do anything in his power to keep me working for him."

"I still don't understand, Jackie… you speak as if your father has some hold over you."

Things were getting difficult and Jackie opted for lying to him. "I am my father's only close relative and I handle many of his business. He could, I suppose, give this side of the business to someone else in the corporation, but he prefers to have me do it. He has taught me everything about the business and because I have always handled everything that he has asked me to do, he believes that no one but me can really do it."

"But it isn't fair to you! Does he want you to do his work forever?"

"Pretty much so, yes…"

He shook his head. "Well, with all due respect to him and to you as his daughter, he's too possessive. He must realize that you may want to get marry and start your own family someday…"

She didn't know how to explain to him that Tony never thought of her as a person but as a machine that could shoot and kill at his will. Her head moved slowly from side to side. "I know he realizes that, Aidan, but up until now I had never felt the need to get away and start a life without all the headaches and demands that my job carries."

"And now you do?" His voice became low.

"Yes. I suddenly started to think more like a woman and not so much as a machine who does a job..." She stood on her toes and placed a small kiss on his lips. "I'm ready to face my father now."

"How long do you need when you get back?"

She looked at her hands on his shoulders and took a moment to answer. "Probably two months, give or take...my attorney can finalize the sale of the building, but I need to think about the furniture in my apartment and a few other things that I can't leave hanging there..."

"And are you sure you want to come back here?"

"I do. That is, if you want me...we can have a trial period and then, if we think we don't want to go on with it I'll move on."

He shook his head as in disbelief. "You are so cool talking about that!"

"Aidan...I'm a very independent woman. I can support myself and live alone if I have to and will never whine about it. You are a wonderful man and the fact that you'd like to have me back here with you fills me with happiness…but it won't kill me if after a while you realize that I'm not the person for you. It will hurt…but as everything, it will pass."

"I can see you are also very proud."

"I have to be, dearest…"

"And I admire you even more for it. So…if you think it's the right thing for you, then go back home, do what you must do and come back. I'll be waiting for you with open arms."

She smiled at him and hugged him tighter, then turned and started to run towards the cottage. "Race you upstairs," she said with a wicked smile.

CHAPTER THIRTEEN

The days passed too fast for Jackie and Aidan. He took her everywhere, she met some of his friends, went to an emergency visit to one of the farms and witnessed the birth of a calf, she visited his friend Patrick O'Faolian, the master craftsman who showed her his show room and had her drooling over his creations, they went to dinner with his parents again, and were daily visitors to the village pub. Every day that passed took her closer to the day she had to say good-bye to him and go back to face Tony – or at least, face the decisions she had made to break away from Tony's control. Aidan thought that her father's business was in the corporate world, and Jackie shuddered at the thought of him finding out the truth. Even so, she stayed with him for two weeks – and each day was better than the one before.

The day finally came when he drove her to Shannon airport for her flight back home. To match their mood, the day was bleak, with a constant rain that didn't stop at all and which seemed to go through her clothing and straight into her very soul. Aidan was also gloomy although she noticed that he was putting out his best face to make her feel better. They stood at the airport security gate and he held her very tight against his chest. "Jackie...I'll ask you just one thing: please come back to Ireland, even if it's a trial thing as you said, but please give us the chance."

She fought tears she hadn't shed in a very long time. "I will, I promise you, Aidan. Give me two months tops, but as we'll be in touch anyway, I'll keep you posted daily of what I'm doing. Trust me."

"I will, I do." He looked at her once more and loosened up his grip, and putting one more kiss on her lips, let her go.

Jackie went through the electronic gates and once she had retrieved her handbag from the plastic container the guard had place it, she looked back and smiled at him. With a last wave, she started to walk towards her gate, and he remained there until she was lost in a turn of the long hallway.

That was the last time they saw each other.

CHAPTER FOURTEEN

O'Hare Airport was busy, as always, but Jackie went through Customs without a cinch. Her squeaky clean passport was a blessing as she didn't have to stop and answer questions from the serious Immigration agents that check visitors into the country every day. A cab took her to her apartment and she went up to her floor in a daze, and once there she called Aidan to let him know she had arrived well.

"I miss you already," she told him. "But I'll start working on my plan today. I'll see if the man downstairs who wanted to buy the building is in and I'll ask him to come to see me. That's the main problem right now. Everything else can be dealt with."

They talked for twenty minutes and when they hung up she sat at her desk. That's when she saw the fax in her machine. It was from Tony and had large letters "call me as soon as you get back!!".

"Crimminy!, what now, Tony?" she said aloud and moved to the telephone again.

"So you're back!" was the first thing Tony said.

"Thank you for missing me, Tony…"

"Lissen Jackie, I'm in no mood for girlie sentiments. Can you come over?"

"No, Tony...I can't! Can you come here instead?"

"Dammit, Jackie..."she heard his voice talking to someone else and waited for him to come back to the line. "Hello, Jackie lissen...we have a problem...this is a biggie, and I need you."

"I just flew in, Tony...can you give me a break?"

"Not this time, Jackie. We have problems in Utah and you have to go out there a.s.a.p."

"Utah? For God's sake, Tony, Utah is out there in the middle of nowhere! Why me?"

"Because you're the only one who can do this."

"Right. I'm the only one...what happened now?"

"It's fucking Senator Melville; he's making noises about giving information to some damn newspaper in Salt Lake City and we need him disposed of."

Disposed of? That's a new phrase for Tony. "That's stupid Tony. Whatever information he gives out is going to link him with us, so I can't believe he'll do anything..."

"Not this time, Jackie...The bastard is writing his memoirs and he already gave all the information to the broad who's doing the work for him."

"Oh, Tony, for God's sake! Memoirs! Who's going to believe him!"

"Who's gonna believe him? Fucking Larry King, that's who. He's gonna appear in his program in two weeks and is gonna tell all."

"Tony...chill out, will you! Who's going to believe that Big Senator Melville is going to appear in national television and tell the entire country that he has been receiving money from us for keeping quiet about...what is it? The landfill bill?"

"Yes, that's the one. He has already told that woman writer about it, so, Jackie, you have to go to Utah and get rid of both. I'm faxing you all the information now as we speak." As if confirming his words, her fax machine rang at that time and she looked at it. His instructions started to spit out of the machine and she automatically reached for them. She could hear Tony's voice saying something else and she put the receiver by her ear again. "Say that again, Tony..."

"I was saying that the Senator is spending a few days in his vacation house in Park City, so you go directly there, but first, I want you to get rid of the bitch and try to get all the papers she's got with his notes. It's all in the instructions, Jackie..."

"I can read. Jeez, Tony…can't I have a day to rest?"

"No, you can't. This has to be done immediately. The limo is going to pick you up in about two hours, and you can read those papers during your flight; you're using the jet."

"Talk to you later, Tony…"

"Thanks, Jackie…I owe you big time, kid."

"Yeah… yadda-yadda-yadda…" and she terminated the call sticking her tongue out at the telephone, like a recalcitrant six-year old. There was no doubt that she had to leave the country without a trace or she'd never get to be anything but the hired killer for the Quaglia organization. Oh, God…how awful if Aidan found out about this part of her life! Was she ever going to be free of it?

She went to her room and unpacked her bags. She washed her clothes, packed a small case for her next trip and fell on her bed wiping tears of frustration from her tired eyes. Damn Tony! Damn, damn, damn him!! A few moments later she heard the doorbell and walked towards the door. Dino was there, his grin lit his handsome face and he gave her a military salute. "Bona sera, carissima…" Good evening, dearest… Darling Dino, always flattering her. "Hola bello mio!" and gave him her best smile and a continental kiss on each cheek. He took her small carrying case and waited until she closed the door, then started the elevator. She made small chat until they reached the basement parking where Tony's limo was waiting with the engine running.

A second trip to O'Hare Airport, this time to the hangar where Tony's jet was waiting for her. She knew she wouldn't be able to sleep because there were quite a few papers she was supposed to memorize, so, as soon as they took off into the black Chicago sky, she sat down to read. Dino had smiled at her and said, "I'll be waiting for you when you get back, Signorina Jackie..." and she had waved at him with a cheerfulness she didn't quite feel.

The name of the woman, a ghostwriter Senator Melville had chosen to write the story of his life, was Molly Mason. I hate alliterative names! thought Jackie, Just for that reason I'll make her suffer! And she gave a small chuckle because she knew very well that she couldn't do it. One rule in her life was to never make them suffer if she could help it.

The woman lived alone in a Salt Lake City neighborhood called Sandy, a bit south of the city, and she used to run every morning before the sun was up. Good tip. Good reading too, but her eyelids felt heavy and her temples were throbbing. Before she could help herself, Jackie closed her eyes for a moment and told herself she'd rest her eyes until she could set them on the paper again, but she felt asleep and was waken up by Rick Milano. He shook her gently and her eyes opened, her hand moving fast to her hip. "It's just me, Jackie...we are in Salt Lake International. I can let you sleep here if you wish..."

"Oh, no Rick...it's fine. I'm so tired I don't even know my name." Shaking her head, she stretched and soon was up. "OK, I'll call Tony for a pick up date. Don't tell him that I plan to sleep all day today; no way I'm taking another job the way I feel right now."

"Can't say that I blame you," Rick helped her with her carrying case walking her out of the plane.

Tony had made reservations for her in the Salt Lake Hilton, but she asked the cab driver to take her to another hotel in town and she was driven to Little America, also in the downtown area. Knowing her father, she knew he'd be checking up on her. Fuck him. Oh, she'd get hell away from him as soon as she got back to Chicago, but she could take another pound or so of shit before riding into the sunset.

She went to bed and slept until four that afternoon. Dinner in the hotel dining room woke her up completely, and by the time she went back to her room, she felt ready for anything.

Park City is one of Utah's most fashionable ski resorts, but there are many people that have summer cabins there and live there all year as well. Apparently Senator Melville had put Tony's money to good use and had purchased a condo in town facing the slopes, and a cabin up in the hills surrounded by green pine trees. He was going to be in the condo for the next three days, so Jackie made her plans to get to him while there.

But first the writer. She went to the hotel lobby and asked the clerk to rent a car for her, and after that was done, she went back to her room and studied the street map the man had given her.

The Mormons that founded Salt Lake City had a good idea when they put street numbers instead of names, so she didn't have problems finding the street where the woman lived. Picking up the car, she drove down State Street to the address where she was supposed to turn left towards the mountains, drove about six blocks and found the apartment complex where the woman had a small condominium. She noticed a small park in the back of the building and figured that the woman jogged there in the mornings. She doubted that anyone would go farther than that when it was still dark outside.

Notes taken, Jackie walked around the park for a moment noticing tall trees and pretty high bushes that were still covered with vegetation. Right by the small gate that served as entrance to the park she saw a bench and a drinking fountain, and walking further away from the building she reached a fence that separated the park from the next street. Good thing. She could park the car there instead of the building parking lot. Timing herself, she walked fast towards the front gate and once there she looked at her Rolex: two minutes. If she ran it would be about one minute or less.

Next, Jackie looked up to the building. There were windows facing the small park, and they all had blinds. She couldn't see anyone looking through them, so she turned around and walked the park one more time, noticing where the trees and bushes were located. The path where the woman most probably ran went at times behind the bushes and other times in front, so she'd plan to get to her in one of the turns behind the bushes so there would be less chances of being seen from the building.

She sat in one of the benches that were hidden from the building by small Aspen trees and made her notes and drawings, and after that was done, she walked back to her car. Her blonde wig was hitting against her back, and the large sunglasses hid half of her pretty face --and the shine of her green eyes.

Back in the hotel, Jackie took yet another wig from her bag and shook it, gave it a brushing and let it hang in the bathroom. She was going to wear that one in the morning, and then the blonde one in Park City. Good thing that she had one of those faces that change completely according to her hairdo, and the use of two different wigs would help her cover her appearance well enough. With a sigh, she went to her bed for a lie-down. Closing her eyes, she brought to her mind Aidan's face and his voice. But before talking to him she wanted to have a chat with her neighbour and tenant, the one who had shown interest in buying the building from her. She took an address book and found the man's name. She tapped her fingers to the table while waiting for the man to answer.

"Hello, Mr. Bateman? This is Jackie Quaglia…"

"Ms. Quaglia! Nice to talk to you!"

"Same here, Mr. Bateman. Listen... I wanted to speak with you because I believe I want to sell the building. You had shown interest in it a couple of months ago and am wondering if you are still thinking about it..."

There was a small silence on the line and then the man said, "Well, yes... I am. I didn't think that you were too keen on it that's why I didn't approach you again..."

"I wasn't at the time, Mr. Bateman, but there has been some changes in my personal life and I have changed my mind."

"Well, good! I'd say we should meet soon. Are you home right now?"

"No, I'm out of town, but I'll give you a ring as soon as I get back."

"I'll be waiting, then. See you!"

"Good-bye, Mr. Bateman. My regards to your wife."

"Thank you."

Good. With that out of the way, she called Aidan's number.

Aidan had just finished a small operation on a cat when his telephone rang. His assistant had gone home early so he took the phone and put it on his shoulder, holding it with his face. "Aidan Cassidy," he said and immediately heard the faint buzz of a long distance call. "Is this Jackie?"

"The very same..." she said and giggled. "I felt suddenly homesick and decided to call you to see how you are."

"A lot better now that I hear your voice," he said in his softest voice.

"Good, good...Busy?"

"Not now. Just finished surgery on Mrs. Murphy's cat and was washing my hands."

"Is he all right?"

"She is fine, yes. Just a case of worms that closed her intestines..."

"Please... spare me the gory details..." she laughed and he chuckled. "I haven't had dinner yet..."

"Are you sure that you want to share your life and your stomach with me? I have stories like these one every day."

"Yes, I am sure. And I can always try some tricks to shut you up when you start talking about them."

"Really? What tricks?"

"They involve hands and lips..."

She heard a sigh. "Jackie...please stop right there. I still have one more patient to see." She heard him laughing softly.

"Well, all right. I'll let you go now, but I'll show no mercy next time. Actually... I was calling to let you know that I just spoke with the man who's interested in my building and he and I are going to meet in a couple of days..."

"Good! Does that mean that the problem is almost solved?"

"You said it... almost solved..."

"That's my girl. So, now, tell me how you are."

"I am fine. Had to travel to Denver as soon as I got home because my father was having fits about one of his accounts..."

"You are in Denver now?"

"Yes," she lied and crossed her fingers. "I'll be here for three more days or so and then I'll be back in Chicago starting the arrangements we spoke about. I'll call you with all the details just as soon as I speak with Mr. Bateman."

"Good. I miss you madly, Jackie, it sounds strange but it seems you left a great empty space within me..."

"And you in me, darling. I'll call you tomorrow again and the next day until I get back. OK with you?"

"Of course. I'll be looking forward to that."

"OK...ah... Aidan...I wanted to ask you something..."

"Carry on, love, you can ask me anything."

"The day we spoke about the financing you can't get from your father, I had an idea...would you accept that I send you the money you need to expand the surgery?"

There was a short silence and then he said, "Jackie...you probably misunderstood the amount that I need. It's just too much money...in fact, I had a talk with Father this morning and I believe he's going to go along with me."

"Aidan...I know how much you need and it doesn't bother me. Please let me be the one to help you. It would mean a lot to me..."

"No, Jackie...two-hundred thousand Irish pounds is a good bundle, even in dollars...I can't possibly allow you to lend me that money."

"Why not?"

There was patience in his voice, but she could also hear determination. "Because it's too large an amount, Jackie darling. I do appreciate your concern to help, but I can't accept it."

"You are nothing but a stubborn Irishman!"

"Yes, I am. And you are nothing but a wonderful, beautiful, all together big-hearted woman, loved with all my soul…but the answer is still no."

She lowered her voice. "If I were there I could convince you…"

He laughed. "And I'd let you try…but at the end it would be still no. Of course, I'd also let you insist again and again using the same methods…"

"Besides stubborn, you are a dirty old vet."

"Guilty as charged…" his laughter made her close her eyes and yearn for his touch.

"All right…I'll let you go now only because you have a patient waiting and may be the kind that bites, but I haven't given up on you. I love you. I miss you like mad…"

"Same here, darling, never doubt it."

"Bye darling; wait for my call tomorrow."

"I will. Bye for now, love."

She put the phone back with a sigh and placed her head on the pillow. She loved to flirt with him over the phone, especially now that they had shared so many intimate moments in Ireland. Oh, come on days and weeks...hurry up and pass me! She closed her eyes and went over her plans for leaving Chicago as soon as she could after going back from Utah.

La Grange, Illinois - same day

Francino and Benito Rossi were having a conversation in the older man's office. Francino was leaning against the desk and said to his father, "The Bitch is in Utah right now, Dad... and Tony's plan is to get rid of a woman writer who is helping some Senator write his memoirs and also the Senator himself-"

Benito interrupted, "Francino, how much did it cost you to find that out?"

"Just three grand, Dad, and believe you me! it's money well spent. As I was saying, those two are goners, but darling Jackie is not coming back to Chicago. It's costing us twenty-five thousand, but the recipient is someone who has her fate in his dirty little hands, and for that money he'll send his own mother to prison."

"Are you sure? That's a lot of dough..."

"It is, Dad, but it's worth every penny. Trust me."

"Yeah, but twenty-five thousand grand?"

"So what? Ask your trusty bookkeeper to find you a nice tax break...not that he hasn't done it before!"

Salt Lake City, Utah – Same time

Jackie's idea some months ago of finding an attorney unknown to Tony had paid off. He'd be able to handle the sale of her properties in the US and only he would have the information of where she was. The man was a high profile attorney that she had found in the Internet, with a not very large office in La Grange but an excellent reputation within the Illinois Bar Association. She had given him a sizable retainer and explained to him – without the details he didn't have to have – that she was leaving the country and didn't want anyone to know it. As she had shown him her fake documentation that had a spotless past, she was sure he had checked her out and found nothing disreputable about Jacqueline Millard, her alter ego.

She slept a dreamless night, still tired from her transatlantic trip and the stress of having still another job to do for her unrelenting father.

CHAPTER FIFTEEN

The next morning Jackie was up at five-thirty. Dressed in dark jeans, gray T-shirt, and with her dark wig in her handbag, she left the hotel being careful not to be seen. She was wearing dark running shoes just in case someone saw her. The drive to Sandy took only fifteen minutes because the streets were almost empty, and when she got to the back of the apartment house belonging to the writer, she parked on the side street, close to where the gate was located.

She took her gun from the handbag, put the wig on and walked quickly to the small gate. She decided to stand by a large bush with red berries about ten feet from the entrance to the park, hoping that the woman would come that way first. She waited more than twenty minutes behind the bush and all of a sudden heard the little gate opening. It was a tall woman that looked like an Amazon that had been just transplanted to Salt Lake City. Closing the gate, the woman leaned on it for a moment and took a series of small jumps as if getting her feet used to her shoes, and started to walk fast towards where Jackie was.

When she was just four feet from Jackie, Jackie stood on her path and without a word, pointed the gun to the woman's head and fired two shots. She fell with half of her body on the path and the other half on the bush, and Jackie, taking her under her arms, moved her all the way into the bush. She then looked around but so no one. She took a plastic coil with a key hanging from it from around the woman's wrist and calmly started to jog towards the back entrance of the apartment house. There wasn't anyone between the back door and the woman's apartment, and Jackie used the key to open the door and go inside. With the gun in her hand just in case, she quickly located the desk with a computer on top, and started to look for a folder with the information about Senator Melville, and when she found it she opened it and looked inside. There were two yellow pads filled with notes, four brown envelopes with papers, and two small cassettes. Putting everything in her bag, Jackie still opened the drawers and looked to see if she had missed anything else, then went to the woman's bedroom and looked around, but there was nothing else that looked as if it belonged in the file.

With a last look around the apartment, Jackie opened the door and silently left the place. The back door was still ajar as she had left it, and she closed it behind her. Then, jogging towards her car, she went back to the hotel. It was only 6:10 AM.

She worked fast. Taking an envelope from her luggage, she put all the papers in it, put Tony's name on it and a P.O. Box in Chicago, and went into the bathroom to shower. She'd send the envelope to Tony by Federal Express to make sure he had all the incriminating information she took from Molly Mason's apartment, and then would travel to Park City to get rid of Senator Melville.

Damn this life, anyway!

The trip to Park City was faster than she thought it'd be and she found the Senator's condo without problems. A fine rain had started to fall and Jackie found a hotel near the condo, thinking that it would be easier for her to make her plan from there and to stalk the condo, as she usually did.

The little hotel was expensive as hell, but well worth the money. Her room faced the main street and she could also see the Senator's condo from her small balcony. At that hour of the day she could see lights on in the two front windows, but as the rain kept falling the sky was taking a nasty gray color. She noticed that the front door was very close to the door of the next apartment and there was no place to hide – anywhere! She looked again through the papers sent by Tony trying to find a way to meet the Senator outside of his condo, and saw that he was a frequent visitor to a small pub called "The Eagle" located on one of the side streets near his place.

The rest of the day was spent walking casually through the streets near the condo and the pub, and she found out that the pub had a small parking lot in the back. The question was, living so close to it, would he use a car? Probably not. Parking in Park City was not the best in the world because the streets are narrow, so, chances are, the man would walk everywhere.

She went to the pub for a quick lunch and was glad to see the Senator sitting in a table near the window, reading a book. She didn't get close to him but studied him. He checked his watch a few times, and got ready to leave around 1:15 PM. Gathering his book, he walked towards the cash register and paid his bill, not giving a second glance to Jackie who was sitting at the bar, very close to the cashier. The man's voice was a bit hoarse and thanked the man at the cash register by name. Jackie put a ten-dollar bill on the counter and got up to leave before him. Once in the street, she walked casually towards the corner and stood by a window to look at some ski parkas on display. She saw the Senator pass by her and turn right, apparently towards his place. She followed him, stopping at windows to look at the displays.

He went to his condo and opened the door with a key that he took from the pocket of the light jacket he was wearing. He slammed the door once inside and Jackie wondered why. Was he angry or bothered at something? Not at his bank account, she was sure…

She needed time and quiet to think about this situation, so she crossed the street and went back to her hotel. She took off the blonde wig she was wearing and sat by the window. The rain had intensified and was now running freely down the street, making people run for shelter. She leaned back on her easy chair and closed her eyes. Aidan's face came to mind but she dismissed him, forcing herself to think about the problem at hand. If she tried to force open the Senator's door someone for sure would see her, so what was left for her to do was to either kill him somewhere else or make his acquaintance so that he'd invite her to the condo.

But how? A few moments later she sat up and took out her wallet from her oversized bag. Looking through it, she found an old press card for the Boston Globe. Aha! That could be the entry ticket to the man's condo, or at least, to get closer to him and get an invitation.

The time was 2:00 PM and she made a decision. Taking the press card, she called the Senator's phone number from Tony's folder. It was a moment before the hoarse voice answered with a deep 'hello'.

She put her sweetie-pie voice. "Hello? Senator Melville? This is Trudy Morris, of the Boston Globe? I'm calling to see if you could grant me an interview for an article we are putting together about your opinion on the President's views and his politics on the Gulf War."

There was a silence on the other end of the line and then his voice sounded bored, "Yet another interview? I'm here on a short vacation, young lady. And would prefer not to be bothered."

The bastard! Doesn't he know that politicians, like movie stars, continue to live thanks to the press and the public? She almost pouted, "Senator, I can imagine you are very busy, but my paper wants to be the first to start with this series of interviews and your name came up as one that people should listen to...It won't be more than fifteen minutes, I promise you..." You'll be dead before you can realize what happened to you...

He couldn't have been too busy because he said, "Well, all right. Are you here in town? I can give you exactly fifteen minutes – and I can assure you I'll time you – so, if you can be here within the next half hour you're on."

"Oh, thank you, Sir...Yes, I'll be there right on time. Let me double check your address..." and she gave him the condo address, and when he agreed she said a perky bye-bye and hung up the phone.

She wore her dark wig and a felt hat with a visor that she placed low on her face, black jeans, and a dark burgundy sweater. With her gun in her handbag, she left the hotel five minutes before the time set by the Senator, and crossed the street. He was probably waiting for her because he opened the door a second after she knocked. He was tall and balding and was smoking a pipe and Jackie could smell the musky scent of its tobacco.

She beamed when she saw him. "Senator Melville? Trudy Morris, Sir, with the Boston Globe."

"And what's a reporter for the Boston Globe doing in Utah?"

"Actually, I'm mixing business and pleasure. It's my vacation time and as I was coming this way, my editor gave me the assignment in one of his rare moments of niceness."

He smiled at her zest and stood aside for her to come in. The condo was larger than it appeared from outside and Jackie's eyes took everything in just a minute. Kitchen right in front of the entrance hallway and a sitting room of sorts to the right. The man asked her to go into the room and he followed her. She sat in one of the club chairs facing him and he took the sofa.

She looked around the room and saw that the blinds were drawn, making the room dimly lit by the outside light. He turned on one of the side lamps and then sat comfortably in the sofa, looking at her. "So, Ms. Morris...I only have a few minutes like I told you. You better start."

Jackie opened her handbag and took out the gun. "Gladly," she said and shot him once between his eyes. He didn't make a noise, just fell backwards in the sofa and remained there. She moved quickly towards the desk she had seen in one corner and in less than five minutes had gone through all of its contents picking up a small notebook that was being held together with a rubber band. With no time to go through it, she put it in her handbag and, with a last look around, left the room. Instead of going to the front door, she moved quietly towards the kitchen and opened the back door that faced a small patio with a fence and gate to the alley. She used it for her gateway and started to walk at a regular pace towards her right, turning to the street to the front of the condo in less than thirty seconds.

She crossed the street and walked the few yards to her hotel and went quickly inside, and once there she took the small book she had taken from the senator's apartment and, together with the gun, put it in a box to be sent to Tony by overnight mail. She walked to the post office and mailed it, and stopped in a small bistro to have a bite to eat before packing her belongings and leaving Park City for good.

Two hours later she was getting ready to leave her room after wiping carefully the surfaces that she knew she had touched – not many because hers was a small room – when she heard a knock on her door. When she opened it she saw two men that had COPS written all over them.

One of them, tall and mean looking, with a face that resembled Jack Palance, said, "Jacqueline Quaglia? You are under arrest for the death of Molly Mason in Salt Lake City."

CHAPTER SIXTEEN

Jackie never thought that that moment would ever came to her life, and all she could do was numbly follow the men to their car. She was taken to the Park City police department and booked, then she was asked to sit in a small square room where the two men that arrested her and one more that looked like a bulldog put papers in front of her and questioned her and took notes. On the way to the police station her mind had gone over everything that she had done since she killed the Mason woman, and was sure that she had left no evidence whatsoever leading to her person. How in the world did they know it was she? She had mailed the paperwork to Tony immediately, as she had done here today and as she did in every case in which there was paperwork involved.

She was wondering what would happen when they found the Senator's body in his condo. She was allowed one phone call and she called Tony who wasn't home. She left message with one of the men that were always guarding him and demanded that Tony made arrangements immediately for her release or for an attorney to get her out on bail. After all passed, she was put in a cell by herself and the next morning all hell broke loose when his maid found the body of Senator Melville.

The same cops came back and questioned her even more but she didn't say anything else. She couldn't eat or sleep and at the end of the third day her beautiful face was haggard. Still no word from Tony and that put her to think. What could have happened that her father was not doing anything to save her? When she wasn't in front of the cops, she was laying on a hard cot in her cell, thinking. She thought about Aidan and what would happen when he didn't hear from her. As she had been using one of her aliases to communicate with him and when they met, she knew that he could never find out what happened to her unless there was some kind of glitch in the system. Still, the time came after a few weeks when the name Aidan took second place in her thoughts. Hell!, chances are she was not going to see him again – or in a long, long time. At that moment, her priorities were to get the best legal representation she could in order to spend the smallest amount of time in that gray institution filled with gray people.

The legal process was long and painful. Without an attorney to represent her in Utah, all she could do was to hire one whose name had been given by the first Legal Aid lawyer that helped her. She had to make arrangements for the man to be paid an enormous amount from her own money and finally, after about two weeks, she had an expensive attorney who visited her many times and took all the information he needed. She denied the charges over and over again; the attorney told her that because of the fact that the information they had was about Molly Mason, who was working closely with Senator Melville on a very serious matter, and the senator himself had been murdered a couple of days later, she was the prime suspect.

The very expensive attorney that handled her case made some deal with the prosecutor because of the fact that the murder weapon had not been recovered. The attorney claimed her innocence because of that reason and because there was no link between Jackie and the dead woman, but the prosecutor was adamant and at the end the powers that be won. Her attorney told her that she would be better off giving out information regarding the person or persons that had sent her to kill the woman, but Jackie's answer had always been the same. The murder of Senator Melville went unsolved – or rather, unproven – and that fact probably saved her from more years in prison or even the death penalty.

After two months of going to court she was sentenced to 5 to 15 years in the Utah State Prison for women – and that time stretched all the way to the end of the 15th year. She was denied parole from the Board of Pardons every time that she had an appointment with them, which was every four years or so. The last four years of her incarceration, Jackie felt she didn't have any more energy to even write a coherent letter to the Board, but her previous life and what she had learned about self-preservation didn't allow her to give up hope.

La Grange, Illinois

Francino's Porsche entered his father's round driveway as if it were, instead, the racetrack at the Indy 500 and he got out of it leaving the door open.

He walked fast to his father's office, whistling a happy tune, and once he opened the door, he announced to Benito: "I just got word from Utah that Jackie has been given fifteen years in the shade."

Benito looked up from what he was doing. "Really?"

"Yes, Father, really! Apparently they didn't have the 100% evidence that they need or she'd have gotten the death penalty, but fifteen years is enough for us." He walked towards the bar and filled two glasses, giving one to his father. "Here, let's drink to the health – or not – of the Quaglia Bitch, may she rot in prison!"

They drank and Francino sat in front of his father's desk and discussed with him everything that he had heard earlier from the prosecutor in Utah.

Utah State Prison, Draper, Utah

Jackie had been in prison for about six years and had completely lost contact with Tony – something that baffled her to no end - until one day when she was sitting in the medical facility's waiting room when a man – another inmate – sitting in front of her, said, "Tony's dead, kid. I just want you to know it."

Jackie just stood there and like a zombie, she started to get up to approach the bench where the man was, but her guard stopped her with a bark, "Sit down, Quaglia!". Jackie sat down but kept looking at the man. Without taking her eyes from him, she said to the guard, "He said something about my father being dead."

The guard turned her head around, a sign that meant 'If I don't look at you I can't hear anything' and Jackie was grateful to her. Looking at the man, she asked him, "Who are you, and how do you know that Tony is dead?"

He looked around and mumbled, "I was put in here to communicate with you." He got a fast look from the guard but nothing was said, so Jackie said, "I'll be damned!"

She knew that anything was possible for Tony or anyone in the family, so questioning the man was not important at the moment. His family was probably being kept on Easy Street while he was in prison.

"Tell me what happened. Fast, either one of us can be called in at any second…"

"Francino Rossi, Benito's older kid, got to Tony about two months ago. He just came in pretending he had business to discuss and when they were left alone in Tony's office, he shot him. Then he went out through the window."

"That window was always kept open," Jackie said inanely, as if that were important at the moment, and the man nodded. "So, what happened next?"

He shrugged. "Nothin'... Marco is probably gonna take his place, but he's in Italy right now."

"Why did Rossi kill Tony?" Funny, she wasn't feeling anything at that time.

"Go figure... unless it was because Tony had said that the Rossi kids were not going to become the head of the family..."

"Who was...?

"Who was what?" the man's head shot up and looked at her.

"Become head of the family, of course." Duh.

"Well, Tony wanted you, but with you being here and all..." he paused and coughed, "I guess Marco."

Well, well... "So tell me, do you have any idea why Tony never contacted me at all in all these years?"

He shrugged again and put his hand on his chest. His cough, when it came, was that of a person who had started to smoke in kindergarten. "According to Giannini, d'you remember him?" Jackie nodded yes and he went on, "Giannini said that when you were caught here you had been framed by Rossi Senior and that Tony had been told that you had left the country just like that. As you always were a little too independent, Tony bought the story..."

"That's bull crap!," her voice was loud enough to get the guard's attention, who rolled her eyes, shook her head, and said, "Come on, Quaglia, you know better than that!"

"Sorry…" she said and went back to the man. "I don't believe a word of it. Tony would have never just bought the story. He'd have moved heaven and earth to find me!"

"A few of us thought that too, kid…but there he was, all of a sudden believing everything that the Rossis said. They showed him copies of tickets to Brazil, even an address in Rio and a phone number. There was also a letter from you telling him that you were fed up and wanted out and not to look for you ever again."

She didn't doubt for a moment that the Rossis had done something like that to Tony. For all his know-how and brusque manners Tony somehow believed almost everything he was told, especially by people like the Rossis who lied so easily they could dupe Saint Peter. "And they just killed him." That was a statement, not a question. The man nodded and kept looking down. "Why are you here in prison?"

"Just aggravated assault. They gave me seven months, but as the jails are crowded they sent me here. More room." Now he started to look at the ceiling.

"You from Illinois?"

"Here and there…my family is in Jersey."

"Can you keep communicating with me? Writing to me maybe, using a third person?" Jackie looked at the guard at that moment and noticed that the woman was paying unusual attention to a fingernail in her otherwise well kept hands.

"Sure…I'll let you know what's going on."

At that moment a nurse came out of one of the two rooms and called Jackie's name. She gave the man a last look and thanked him with her eyes while walking towards the doctor's office. He didn't acknowledge her look and kept staring at the ceiling.

Through the man, Jackie had been kept abreast of what was happening in Illinois – not as often as he had promised, but she did receive news every few months, but news was not really what she needed. What she wanted and needed was a way out of the prison.

After time passed, she changed her mind and realized that getting out through the gates was a lot more desirable than jumping over the barbed wire, so she sat and waited, but always kept the hope alive that one day the family would pull some of the many strings she knew they could pull and get an early release.

It never happened, and one day, about five days short of her 15th anniversary in prison, she heard her name called through the intercom and they told her to "roll up". She looked at the door of her cell and then at the ceiling and instead of getting her belongings together, she sat on her cot and cried her eyes out. She didn't even know that someone had sent a suit for her to wear that day. She had a couple of interviews with the Adult Probation and Parole offices in Salt Lake City to give information of where she was going to live after being paroled, and she gave Tony's address wishing to keep her apartment in Shore Lake Drive off record, giving also the name of Tony's attorney.

She went through the process of being released as if in a dream. Many of her fellow inmates were there with her hugging her and wishing her good luck, and she accepted all those well wishes with a smile, but her senses were set on the outside world, mostly Chicago.

Jackie Quaglia was free. Although the paperwork was incredible, she knew that after the last signature she'd be able to walk away from the place. She had paid her debt to society, as the social workers would say, but the way she saw it, she was getting the fuck out – never to return!

CHAPTER SEVENTEEN

Chicago, Illinois

Her conversation with Marco in the Big House stuck to her brain and from that day on she started to work towards her complete freedom. Marco and his affiliates faked her death and the doctor that had been working for the family for so many years signed a death certificate stating that Jacqueline Quaglia, age 42, had died of hepatitis. Jackie's skin crawled at the word hepatitis because of the many cases she had seen while in prison, but left it at that. Then, the funeral home had paperwork ready showing that her body had been cremated two days after her death. The attorney presented those papers to the Adult Probation and Parole Department in Chicago and they erased her names from their files without a second glance.

Jackie stayed at the Elmhurst house while that was being arranged, and about a week later received a call from Marco telling her that Dr. Moscowitz was ready to perform the surgery in her hands. She was not looking forward to that, but the man had anesthetized her hands and used a laser beam to erase her fingerprints. It didn't take long and she didn't feel any pain at the moment, and with the pills he gave her, she kept herself drugged until the pain that came later on passed. During those days, she started to make arrangements in

Switzerland with her bank in Zurich to find her an attorney to work with her.

She also started to make other plans, something that she felt she had to do for Tony, although God knows he didn't deserved her thoughts, but he had been her father after all.

Jackie's fingers were still bandaged but she could use her hands. She started to pack her belongings slowly, putting her most precious possessions in large crates that would be shipped ahead of time to Switzerland, in charge of Attorney Etienne Juillard in Bern, the attorney found by her bank, and made all the arrangements with him to locate for her a small villa in the area. She was glad to receive information of the villa in a small town called Murren, about 10 miles south of Interlaken. Self-preservation told her that she should not live anywhere too close to a well-known city because she could meet someone from her old life. The attorney explained to her that the town was not accessible to traffic and people had to drive as far as Stechelberg, the last town on the Lauterbrunner Valley, and from there take a cable car into Murren for a ten minute trip. That was exactly what Jackie needed and she immediately jumped at the chance of buying the small cottage that the attorney had found. The bank had all the paperwork ready to pay for the place through the attorney; Jackie communicated with him almost daily and was ready to take ownership of a smallish place right on the shores of a very small lake.   The many photographs of the outside and inside of the small cottage / chalet had seemed quite charming and she was looking forward to taking possession of the place.

Plans for the future were still on the lap of the gods. She planned to stay there for as long as her visa permitted and then apply for another visa while working on papers to become a resident. Monsieur Juillard had all the information given by her and was working on the papers, but it would take time, she knew.

Sometimes, while waiting for a light to change or for water to boil, she'd wonder about Aidan, and the thought that bothered her most was what did he think when he never heard from her again. Did he think that she was a tease that led him to love her and then disappeared into the sunset? Probably. Any man would. She wished she could somewhat contact him and clear up between them, but what do you say to a man who trusted you and was suddenly cut off from your life? Sorry Aidan, but you see...my father sent me to a place to kill a man and the cops were waiting for me outside. Tough luck, uh? So...can we start where we left off?

Life was more than tough and her mistakes, together with Tony's, were paid in the worst manner fifteen years ago. Jackie only had the future to look forward now. Her past life and past mistakes were just that: past, and better forgotten. More than ever she believed that the old English saying she had heard some time ago was right: Old sins cast long shadows. Yes, her sins were old and had started a long time ago, and their shadows had engulfed her life. Her past life.

The day before leaving Chicago

She had never been more careful than this time to cover her tracks and was sure that nobody could ever find her. Marco had indeed come forward when he had the facial surgeon erase her fingerprints with the thought of having her back in the swing of things for the family, and as Jackie went along with his ideas, he never thought that she'd be gone one day without a second word. The fact that her death had been faked pleased her very much as she knew that Marco and the family wouldn't be able to claim it had been a bogus death because they'd be digging their own graves.

An entire life left behind would probably be too much for any other person to handle, but Jackie's life had hardened her in such a way that this was just a transitory step into something new, something that would last for the rest of her life.

The day before her scheduled flight Jackie left the house wearing dark glasses and a bag that she hanged from her shoulder. She told one of the men in the hall that she was going shopping and would be back in about two hours. When she got to the street she walked two blocks to a shopping center in Elmhurst and from there called a cab. She gave an address in La Grange and sat back in her seat. Her dark glasses were hiding her eyes but her hands were caressing the bag, as if soothing the back of an ailing child.

When they got to La Grange, she told the driver to leave her in a Holiday Inn that she saw from the distance and knew it was close to the place where she wanted to go. Remembering the old rule of never giving large tips, she paid the taxi with a twenty and told the driver to keep the change. He never looked at her in the face because the ball game on the radio was keeping his attention.

She knew that the Rossis still lived in the large house right between the borders of La Grange and Countryside, and although there had been many changes in fifteen years, the walk wasn't too long. She started to walk fast towards the street where her nemesis lived and soon found herself in front of the iron gate that guarded their slimy lives.

Before leaving the house in Elmhurst she had checked with Marco and knew that Benito, the father and capo of the Rossi clan was meeting with Francino, his eldest son and the one who had killed Tony, in the house this day. Marco had given her this information without realizing that she had plans for both men. She didn't care if Marco realized later where the information had come from because she'd be far away from Chicago. She walked towards the large double doors and knocked and was surprised to see Francino opening it. He had gained weight and looked like a pimp in a disco dance. He didn't recognize her at the beginning, and when she asked about Benito he started to give her some excuse that his father wasn't available.

"Cut the crap, Francino, I know he's available and I'd like to speak with him…and with you too."

"Just a minute…" he started and then suddenly realized who she was. "Jackie! I'll be damned! I thought you were in the clink in Idaho…"

"Yes, it's me…and it wasn't Idaho, it was Utah."

"Same difference," said the bastard. "What do you want with me and my father?"

"Just a small talk. Where is he?"

"He's in the library, but he's busy."

"Tell him to free himself for just ten minutes. He'll be interested to hear what I have to tell you both."

He looked at her for a moment before stepping aside to let her in. Jackie's trained eyes took everything in the room and saw that there were no henchmen sitting around the place and, walking towards the door on her left, entered the library. She saw Benito Rossi sitting behind his desk, his large frame taking the entire back of the piece of furniture. Jackie looked around the room. They were alone.

"Hello Benito! Long time no see."

"Well, Jackie…" he got up and started to walk towards her. "This is a surprise…"

"I bet it is…I just want a moment with you and Francino here, if you don't mind. I won't take too much of your time."

"You got business with us, Jackie? I thought that after Tony died, God rests his soul, Marco was in charge..."

"Yes, Marco is in charge in spite of your wishes...but let's leave that aside, Benito, I don't care who is in charge now. I just want to clear the air between us."

Benito looked at her for a moment. "OK, but let's have a drink, OK Jackie? Francino, gets us something to drink."

If he was asking Francino to fix the drink Jackie figured they were alone in the house, so she turned around and said, "Don't worry Francino, this is too early for drinks. Let's just chat."

She sat herself in one of the chairs facing the desk and motioned Francino to the other one. Benito went back to his large chair behind the desk.

"OK," she started, looking at them, "first of all, let me make something clear...I'm not blaming you for Tony's death. I know you shot him, Francino, but to tell you the truth, after the way he left me in prison for all these years without moving a finger to get me out...well, it's hard to love someone who does that to you, even though that someone is one's own father. That's not why I'm here today. I understand that I actually went to prison because someone framed me. Someone..." he looked from father to son, " told Tony a cockeyed story about me going to Brazil, even showed him a letter that I supposedly left for him... Do you two happen to know who did that?" her green eyes were as dangerous as a panther's.

The two men looked at each other but was Benito the one who spoke. "And who told you all those stories, Jackie? That Francino shot Tony?"

"What difference does it make? In fact, I found out while still in prison, a few months after it happened..." She moved in the chair in order to make herself more comfortable. "But really...don't you think it's time to clear the air between us? It really stinks."

Another silence followed, so she continued, "I want to know why. It has bothered me for many years..."

Benito cleared his throat. "What happened between us, Jackie, was a man thing..."

"A man thing? What does that mean, Benito? That we women are not intelligent enough to understand?" Her voice rose when she asked the question and the two men flinched.

"No, Jackie...take it easy... What I meant was that there was a misunderstanding between Tony and us Rossis... Francino lost his temper and shot Tony."

"Just like that?" She looked at Francino when she said that.

"Well, yeah...Tony got antsy with me..."

"So you kill people just because they get 'antsy' with you?"

"Well, yeah...it was more than that, Jackie...Tony would not listen to reason..."

Her eyes became slits and Francino moved in his chair. She finally said, "I see..." and looked at Benito, "I think I'll accept a drink now, Benito, but just water, please." She wanted to see if she called someone to bring the water, but again, Benito looked at Francino. "There's fresh Evian water over there, Francino, bring Jackie a glass..."

She realized that if Benito was asking his son to fetch the water then they were alone in the house. She wanted to be extra sure of this. When Francino made the motion to get up, she took her pistol from her bag and said, "I changed my mind again. It's a woman thing, you know? Sit down Francino!"

When Francino sat down, she added, "And don't you even dream with moving your hands because you'll be history. Now... I lived fifteen years in prison because the two of you put me there. Not only you told Tony stories about me, you also tried your best to occupy the place that was rightfully mine in the Quaglia organization..."

"The place is yours, Jackie... I don't want it!" Francino's forehead was shiny with perspiration.

"I don't want it either, Francino... After I leave this house today I'm going to be completely free of this life and of you... Tony didn't deserve to die the way he did , and for that reason you are going to pay…" she lifted the gun when she noticed Francino was going to stand up, "sit down!" she said and then she looked down and to Francino's humiliation, she started to laugh when she noticed that the younger man had peed his pants. A large wet stain was spreading rapidly downwards. "You are not only a fucking coward, Francino, you are a sissy to boot! I bet you like boys too…"

When Francino tried to answer, she just moved the gun up a bit and shot him on the forehead.

Benito's face was blank. Jackie then turned to him and said, "I'm sure that your brainless son did what you told him to do, Benito, therefore you are as guilty as he is," and shot him as well.

Her pistol had a silencer and she didn't believe anyone had heard the shots, but just in case… Getting up fast, she looked around the chair making sure she hadn't dropped anything, and left the library as fast as she could. She closed the door behind her and did the same with the front door, and crossed the garden with long strides. Once outside the iron gates, she looked behind but saw no movement in the house. She walked fast a couple of blocks and found a taxi right in front of a small motel, took it and asked to be driven to the same shopping mall near the house in Elmhurst.

She called Marco as soon as she got back to the house and, still covering her tracks, made up a story about falling asleep and asked him if she could see him the next day at six PM. By that time she'd be somewhere over the Atlantic, but wanted her cousin to believe she was still in town.

She went to her dresser and started to put some small things in a carry-on, then, after taking her three guns which she wrapped in plastic, she walked to the basement of the house where an incinerator was located and threw them there. With the clank she heard at the bottom of the incinerator, she closed that portion of her life and walked back upstairs. About two hours later she left the house once more and checked in at the O'Hare Hilton for her flight to Switzerland via Washington DC and Paris.

When the plane took off the next day near noon, she didn't even look down at Chicago the way she used to do in the past. She closed her eyes and let the big city and the blue Lake Michigan behind.

Murren, Switzerland - One month later

Sitting alone in the small village inn, she was waiting for her meal and reminiscing the last days spent in Chicago. Marco had expected her to go back to work as soon as possible, but she had insisted in having the surgeon work on her hands before she took on another job. "Marco," she had said to her cousin, "I'm not going to put my freedom in danger by going to another job so soon And besides," she had added," I have to practice; maybe I could go to the shooting range a couple of days a week. Remember I haven't shot anything for fifteen fucking years!" Marco had understood and granted her the time she claimed she needed. The truth is, she knew that was just a cover story as she could have shot and killed a midget hiding behind a bush with her left hand, but she needed to make time. That procedure was needed before she tackled her last job of killing the Rossis.

Making the arrangements with her Swiss bank and newly found attorney in Bern had been easy. Her passport was returned to her within 10 days thanks to the "urgent" paragraph she put in the application together with the fake itinerary she had gotten from her travel agent for a trip that she cancelled right after the passport arrived. Jacqueline Millard had made the trip from Chicago to Washington DC on United and from there to Paris via Air France. In Paris she had taken a train to Bern and now she was already in Murren, one of those places that when passing through it, if you blink your eyes you miss it. Her beautiful auburn hair was now light brown and she had blue contact lenses.

When she arrived in Bern she contacted the attorney and the older man made arrangements for the crates with furniture and other belongings to be delivered to her as soon as possible. That still took longer than she wanted because of the difficult location chosen by her, but after a few long weeks everything was in the new cottage.

The place was more than charming. It had two bedrooms under the eaves separated by a complete bathroom, and downstairs a large room with a fireplace large enough to roast an ox, sitting room with a bay window, kitchen, another small bath, and a pantry almost as large as the kitchen. She had bought a state-of-the-art computer with laser printer and had plenty of paper and cartridges to last her at least six months. Winters were longer than anywhere else in this valley and she didn't want to run out of supplies. She was going to start writing about her life, not a biography, but a fictional novel that would attract the attention of a publisher. She had the education to do it and knew that she could easily do it.

She turned the sitting room into a charming office with all the amenities she knew she would need. With a new life starting again, Jackie was looking forward to creating the existence that she deserved after all those years in prison. Nobody would ever know who she really was, and if anybody ever found out…well, let him, or her, prove it.

Going through her bank papers one day in Chicago, she was surprised to find out that four years after she went to prison, there had been a deposit of three million dollars to her account. She called the bank and asked the president himself information regarding that deposit. The man had to ask her the zillion questions they ask in cases like this to prove that it was indeed herself and she sat down when the man said that it came from the account of an Anthony Quaglia in Chicago. The money had been put in Jackie's Citybank account, an account she had under her own name and her alias Jacqueline Millard as a beneficiary, and when Ms. Millard transferred the account to Switzerland, the three million dollars had transferred along – together with all the interests earned in eleven years.

"So," she said to herself at the time, "Tony had indeed come through somehow but not with a lawyer to get me out but as always, with money to cover his mistakes." She shrugged. "The matter of never knowing why Tony had never contacted me in prison will bother me forever, but all is well that ends well. The bastard owned me that and a lot more! But he and I are even now. The Rossis are dead."

She wondered what was going on in Chicago, but she'd find out as soon as the subscription of the Chicago Tribune started to arrive. She could also buy USA Today in Bern and planned to do that during her first trip there.

When her meal came she thanked the young woman who delivered it and started to eat, worries left behind, and the promise of a future that only she could change if she wanted to.

Note from the Author

'Jackie' is real. The personality shown in this writing is hers; her sense of humor is always present, even in her darkest days; and her love/hate for 'Tony' is there when she talks. How can one explain a personality like hers without two or three degrees in Psychology? I know I can't, but I met this woman and I know that – for better or for worse – this is the way she lived.

I always felt that the story is not quite finished because I'll always question the reason why 'Tony' never helped her when she was arrested, but, if she knows the truth herself, she has her own reasons for not telling it at this time.

The proverbial 'names and places have been changed to protect the innocent' is present in every page, but the uncanny episodes that depict the life of a charming woman who grew up trying to please her ruthless father... those are true. 'Jackie' read every one of these chapters, made the changes she felt necessary, and always sent me comments that helped me get into her mind and supported me in every way throughout the writing. There would be no story without her, and to her I'll always be grateful.